AMERICAN HUMORISTS SERIES

IN PASTURES NEW

George Ade

LITERATURE HOUSE / GREGG PRESS

Upper Saddle River, N. J.

Republished in 1969 by
LITERATURE HOUSE
an imprint of The Gregg Press
121 Pleasant Avenue
Upper Saddle River, N. J. 07458

Standard Book Number—8398-0054-1
Library of Congress Card—74-91072

Printed in United States of America

THE AMERICAN HUMORISTS

Art Buchwald, Bob Hope, Red Skelton, S. J. Perelman, and their like may serve as reminders that the "cheerful irreverence" which W. D. Howells, two generations ago, noted as a dominant characteristic of the American people has not been smothered in the passage of time. In 1960 a prominent Russian literary journal called our comic books "an infectious disease." Both in Russia and at home, Mark Twain is still the best-loved American writer; and Mickey Mouse continues to be adored in areas as remote as the hinterland of Taiwan. But there was a time when the mirthmakers of the United States were a more important element in the gross national product of entertainment than they are today. In 1888, the British critic Grant Allen gravely informed the readers of the *Fortnightly*: "Embryo Mark Twains grow in Illinois on every bush, and the raw material of *Innocents Abroad* resounds nightly, like the voice of the derringer, through every saloon in Iowa and Montana." And a half-century earlier the English reviewers of our books of humor had confidently asserted them to be "the one distinctly original product of the American mind"—"an indigenous home growth." Scholars are today in agreement that humor was one of the first vital forces in making American literature an original entity rather than a colonial adjunct of European culture.

The American Humorists Series represents an effort to display both the intrinsic qualities of the national heritage of native prose humor and the course of its development. The books are facsimile reproductions of original editions hard to come by—some of them expensive collector's items. The series includes examples of the early infiltration of the autochthonous into the stream of jocosity and satire inherited from Europe but concentrates on representative products of the outstanding practitioners. Of these the earliest in point of time are the exemplars of the Yankee "Down East" school, which began to flourish in the 1830's— and, later, provided the cartoonist Thomas Nast with the idea for Uncle Sam, the national personality in striped pants. The series follows with the chief humorists who first used the Old Southwest as setting. They were the founders of the so-called frontier humor.

The remarkable burgeoning of the genre during the Civil War period is well illustrated in the books by David R. Locke, "Bill Arp," and others who accompanied Mark Twain on the way to fame in the jesters' bandwagon. There is a volume devoted to Abraham Lincoln as jokesmith and spinner of tall tales. The wits and satirists of the Gilded Age, the Gay Nineties, and the first years of the present century round out the sequence. Included also are several works which mark the rise of Negro humor, the sort that made the minstrel show the first original contribution of the United States to the world's show business.

The value of the series to library collections in the field of American literature is obvious. And since the subjects treated in these books, often with surprising realism, are intimately involved with the political and social scene, and the Civil War, and above all possess sectional characteristics, the series is also of immense value to the historian. Moreover, quite a few of the volumes carry illustrations by the ablest cartoonists of their day, a matter of interest to the student of the graphic arts. And, finally, it should not be overlooked that the specimens of Negro humor offer more tangible evidence of the fixed stereotyping of the Afro-American mentality than do the slave narratives or the abolitionist and sociological treatises.

The American Humorists Series shows clearly that a hundred years ago the jesters had pretty well settled upon the topics that their countrymen were going to laugh at in the future—from the Washington merry-go-round to the pranks of local hillbillies. And as for the tactics of provoking the laugh, these old masters long since have demonstrated the art of titillating the risibilities. There is at times mirth of the highbrow variety in their pages: neat repartee, literary parody, Attic salt, and devastating irony. High seriousness of purpose often underlies their fun, for many of them wrote with the conviction that a column of humor was more effective than a page of editorials in bringing about reform or combating entrenched prejudices. All of the time-honored devices of the lowbrow comedians also abound: not only the sober-faced exaggeration of the tall tale, outrageous punning, and grotesque spelling, but a boisterous Homeric joy in the rough-and-tumble. There may be more beneath the surface, however, for as one of their number, J. K. Bangs, once remarked, these old humorists developed "the exuberance of feeling and a resentment of restraint that have helped to make us the free and independent people that we are." The native humor is indubitably American, for it is infused with the customs, associations, convictions, and tastes of the American people.

PROFESSOR CLARENCE GOHDES
Duke University
January, 1969   *Durham, North Carolina*

GEORGE ADE

George Ade, journalist, playwright, satirist, and fabulist, was born in Kentland, Indiana, in 1866, and died in Brook, Indiana, in 1944. He studied science at Purdue and received his B. S. in 1887. He then worked for three years on Lafayette, Indiana, newspapers. In 1890 he went to Chicago, the city that he later characterized as a mining camp five stories high. He was hired by the *Morning News* (renamed the *Record* shortly thereafter), and plunged into the life of the brutally competitive, yet exciting and optimistic city which was to furnish him with the subject matter for his stories and fables. In 1893 the characters of Doc' Horne, Artie, and Pink Marsh began to appear in his columns called "All Roads Lead to the Fair" and "Stories of the Street and Town." Ade's early sketches—shrewd, realistic, sometimes nostalgic—describe the experiences of small-town people like himself who try to cope, with varying degrees of success, with big-city life. As Edmund Wilson puts it: "George Ade is like an up-to-the-minute uncle who has been getting on well in the city and who has come back to see the family in the country." He good-naturedly mocks the false sophistication and cultural pretensions of the metropolis, and the narrowness and naiveté of the town, but neither is attacked with bitterness.

Ade's first book, *Artie* (1896), evolved from his newspaper column. This is a gently humorous story which centers about the escapades of a gauche young clerk who wishes to be a lady-killer and young-man-about-town. This was followed by *Pink Marsh* (1897), which contains social criticism interspersed with its humor. Pink Marsh is a Negro bootblack who on one occasion states: "We got mo' rights 'an anybody, but it sutny ain't safe to use 'em." *Doc' Horne* (1899) returns to the world of the white lower-middle class, and takes place in a boarding house in which the good doctor, as resident philosopher and gentle shepherd to lost souls, dispenses wisdom to anyone who will listen.

It was in these early stories and sketches that Ade developed his ear for the richness of everyday American speech: "The language talked by the inhabitants of Crane's *Maggie* is a patently invented lingo when set next to the vernacular of Ade's characters" is the enthusiastic and accurate comment of Larzer Ziff. And a contemporaneous critic called Ade "the Shakespeare of Slang."

There is little disagreement that the "Fables in Slang" are his finest work. There is nothing that dates faster than humor, but the fables are as fresh today as they were a half a century ago. They are not, in spite of the title, written in slang; on the contrary they have a very high degree of literary sophistication. The language is picturesque and filled with racy colloquialisms, but is never inaccessible. When an outmoded word occasionally appears, it is easy to decipher it from the context. The short, exquisitely turned sentences are the opposite of the involutions of Finley Peter Dunne. Ade discovered a simple but magically effective device—capitalization—for making shopworn nouns and adjectives take on new life.

The first "Fable" appeared in 1898, supposedly because he had run out of ideas for his column in the *Record*. It was called "The Blond Girl Who Married a Bucket Shop Owner," and it set the pattern for a series of fables which appeared, about one a week, for the next ten years.

Some of the "Fables" were collected and published in 1899. They were well received by the public, and a second series, *More Fables,* appeared the next year, followed by *Forty Modern Fables* (1902), and *The Girl Proposition* (also 1902).

Ade had always been in love with the theater, and while continuing to write fiction and fables, turned out a satirical comic opera, *The Sultan of Sulu,* based upon his visit to Hadji Mohammed, ruler of the Sulu Islands. This operetta had a long run on Broadway. *The County Chairman* (1903) ridiculed small-town politicians. *The College Widow* (1904), called "one of the theater's indestructibles," is a farce which pokes fun at the absurdities of American collegiate life—especially "football fever."

In Pastures New (1906) is a priceless work for those who enjoy the contemplation of the perennial spectacle of the American provincial in Europe and the Orient: the "easy mark" who is King in his home town but, according to Ade, resembles raw meat on its way to the zoo when he ventures out of his bailiwick. Ade's comments upon the agonies of communication are extremely funny: "The Arabic language, when spoken, sounds very much like an agitated person trying to dislodge a fish bone," and the dialects spoken in the British Isles receive some good-natured spoofing. If one insists upon taking seriously a book which was intended to make the reader laugh, there are psychologically astute sketches of the inhibited, Puritanical American regarding with envy the "vices" of the European capitals, and one encounters caricatures of the "innocent" Americans of Henry James. But Ade, whose freewheeling "wise-guy" approach to life has much in common with Henry Miller's, never holds his countrymen up to ridicule: they are no more or less corrupt and absurd than the French or English shopkeeper who bilks them. And there is even something approaching pathos in the story of the fall of the American Consul, the good Eben Willoughby from Michigan, who disgraces himself because he tries to be too democratic.

PRINCIPAL WORKS: *Artie*, 1896; *Pink Marsh*, 1897; *Doc' Horne*, 1899; *Fables in Slang*, 1900; *More Fables*, 1900; *Forty Modern Fables*, 1901; *The Girl Proposition*, 1902; *People You Know*, 1903; *In Babel*, 1903; *Breaking Into Society*, 1903; *True Bills*, 1904; *In Pastures New*, 1906; *The Slim Princess*, 1907; *Knocking the Neighbors*, 1912; *Ade's Fables*, 1914; *Hand-Made Fables*, 1920; *Single Blessedness*, 1922; *Bang! Bang!* 1928; *The Old-Time Saloon*, 1931; *Thirty Fables*, 1933.

ADDITIONAL WORKS: *Stories of the Streets and of the Town* (ed. F. J. Meine), 1941; *The Permanent Ade* (ed. F. C. Kelly), 1947. Plays—*The Sultan of Sulu*, 1902; *Peggy from Paris*, 1903; *The County Chairman*, 1903; *The Sho-Gun*, 1904; *The College Widow*, 1904; *The Bad Samaritan*, 1905; *Just Out of College*, 1905; *Marse Covington*, 1906; *Mrs. Peckham's Carouse*, 1906; *Father and the Boys*, 1907; *The Fair Co-Ed*, 1908; *The Old Town*, 1909, *Nettie*, 1914.

Upper Saddle River, N. J.   F. C. S.
May, 1969

IN PASTURES NEW

Holds it the same as a slide trombone

IN PASTURES NEW

BY

GEORGE ADE

NEW YORK
McCLURE, PHILLIPS & CO.
MCMVI

Many of the letters appearing in this volume were printed in a syndicate of newspapers in the early months of 1906. With these letters have been incorporated extracts from letters written to the Chicago Record in 1895 and 1898. For the use of the letters which first appeared in the Chicago Record, acknowledgment is due Mr. Victor F. Lawson.

CONTENTS

In London

CONTENTS

In Cairo

IN LONDON

CHAPTER I

GETTING ACQUAINTED WITH THE ENGLISH LANGUAGE

IT may be set down as a safe proposition that every man is a bewildered maverick when he wanders out of his own little bailiwick. Did you ever see a stock broker on a stock farm, or a cow puncher at the Waldorf?

A man may be a large duck in his private puddle, but when he strikes deep and strange waters he forgets how to swim.

Take some captain of industry who resides in a large city of the Middle West. At home he is unquestionably IT. Everyone knows the size of his bank account, and when he rides down to business in the morning the conductor of the trolley holds the car for him. His fellow passengers are delighted to get a favouring nod from him. When he sails into the new office building the elevator captain gives him a cheery but deferential " good morning." In his private office he sits at a $500 roll top desk from Grand Rapids, surrounded by push buttons, and

3

when he gives the word someone is expected to hop. At noon he goes to his club for luncheon. The head waiter jumps over two chairs to get at him and relieve him of his hat and then leads him to the most desirable table and hovers over him even as a mother hen broods over her first born.

This Distinguished Citizen, director of the First National Bank, trustee of the Cemetery Association, member of the Advisory Committee of the Y. M. C. A., president of the Saturday Night Poker Club, head of the Commercial Club, and founder of the Wilson County Trotting Association, is a whale when he is seated on his private throne in the corn belt. He rides the whirlwind and commands the storm. The local paper speaks of him in bated capital letters, and he would be more or less than human if he failed to believe that he was a very large gun.

Take this same Business Behemoth and set him down in Paris or Rome or Naples. With a red guide book clutched helplessly in his left hand and his right hand free, so that he can dig up the currency of the realm every thirty seconds, he sets forth to become acquainted with mediæval architecture and the work of the old masters. He is just as helpless and apprehensive as a country boy at Coney

4

Island. The guides and cabmen bullyrag him. News-boys and beggars pester him with impunity. Children in the street stop to laugh at his **Kansas City** hat known to the trade as a Fedora. When he goes into a shop the polite brigand behind the showcase

Stop to laugh at his Kansas City hat

charges him two prices and gives him bad money for change.

Why? Because he is in a strange man's town, stripped of his local importance and battling with a foreign language. The man who cannot talk back immediately becomes a weakling.

What is the chief terror to travel? It is the lonesomeness of feeling that one cannot adapt himself to the unfamiliar background and therefore is sure to attract more or less attention as a curio. And in what city does this feeling of lonesomeness become most overwhelming? In London.

The American must go to England in order to learn for a dead certainty that he does not speak the English language. On the Continent if he kicks on the charges and carries a great deal of hand luggage and his clothes do not fit him any too well he may be mistaken for an Englishman. This great joy never awaits him in London.

I do not wish to talk about myself, yet I can say with truthfulness that I have been working for years to enrich the English language. Most of the time I have been years ahead of the dictionaries. I have been so far ahead of the dictionaries that sometimes I fear they will never catch up. It has been my privilege to use words that are unknown to Lindley Murray. Andrew Lang once started to read my works and then sank with a bubbling cry and did not come up for three days.

It seems that in my efforts to enrich the English language I made it too rich, and some who tried it afterward complained of mental gastritis. In one of my fables, written in pure and undefiled Chicago,

6

reference was made to that kind of a *table d'hôte* restaurant which serves an Italian dinner for sixty cents. This restaurant was called a "spaghetti joint." Mr. Lang declared that the appellation was altogether preposterous, as it is a well-known fact that spaghetti has no joints, being invertebrate and quite devoid of osseous tissue, the same as a caterpillar. Also he thought that "cinch" was merely a misspelling of "sink," something to do with a kitchen. Now if an American reeking with the sweet vernacular of his native land cannot make himself understood by one who is familiar with all the ins and outs of our language, what chance has he with the ordinary Londoner, who gets his vocabulary from reading the advertisements carried by sandwich men?

This pitiful fact comes home to every American when he arrives in London—there are two languages, the English and the American. One is correct; the other is incorrect. One is a pure and limpid stream; the other is a stagnant pool, swarming with bacilli. In front of a shop in Paris is a sign, "English spoken—American understood." This sign is just as misleading as every other sign in Paris. If our English cannot be understood right here in England, what chance have we among strangers?

IN PASTURES NEW

One of the blessed advantages of coming here to England is that every American, no matter how old he may be or how often he has assisted at the massacre of the mother tongue, may begin to get a correct line on the genuine English speech. A few Americans, say fifty or more in Boston and several in New York, are said to speak English in spots. Very often they fan, but sometimes they hit the ball. By patient endeavor they have mastered the sound of " a " as in " father," but they continue to call a clerk a clerk, instead of a " clark," and they never have gained the courage to say " leftenant." They wander on the suburbs of the English language, nibbling at the edges, as it were. Anyone living west of Pittsburg is still lost in the desert.

It is only when the Pilgrim comes right here to the fountain head of the Chaucerian language that he can drink deep and revive his parched intellect. For three days I have been camping here at the headwaters of English. Although this is my fourth visit to London and I have taken a thorough course at the music halls and conversed with some of the most prominent shopkeepers on or in the Strand, to say nothing of having chatted almost in a spirit of democratic equality with some of the most representative waiters, I still feel as if were a little child playing by the seashore while the great ocean of British idioms lies undiscovered before me.

Yesterday, however, I had the rare and almost delirious pleasure of meeting an upper class Englishman. He has family, social position, wealth, several capital letters trailing after his name (which is long enough without an appendix), an ancestry, a glorious past and possibly a future. Usually an American has to wait in London eight or ten years before he meets an Englishman who is not trying to sell him dress shirts or something to put on his hair. In two short days—practically at one bound—I had realised the full ambition of my countrymen.

Before being presented to the heavy swell I was taken into the chamber of meditation by the American who was to accompany me on this flight to glory. He prepared me for the ceremony by whispering to me that the chap we were about to meet went everywhere and saw everybody; that he was a 'varsity man and had shot big game and had a place up country, and couldn't remember the names of all his clubs—had to hire a man by the year just to remember the names of his clubs.

May I confess that I was immensely flattered to know that I could meet this important person? When we are at long range we throw bricks at the aristocracy and landed gentry, but when we come close to them we tremble violently and are much

Just to remember the names of his clubs

pleased if they differentiate us from the furniture of the room.

Why not tell the truth for once? I was tickled

and overheated with bliss to know that this social
lion was quite willing to sit alongside of me and
breathe the adjacent atmosphere.

Also I was perturbed and stage frightened because
I knew that I spoke nothing but the American language, and that probably I used my nose instead of
my vocal chords in giving expression to such
thoughts as might escape from me. Furthermore,
I was afraid that during our conversation I might
accidentally lapse into slang, and I knew that in
Great Britain slang is abhorred above every other
earthly thing except goods of German manufacture.
So I resolved to be on my guard and try to come as
near to English speech as it is possible for anyone
to come after he has walked up and down State
street for ten years.

My real and ulterior motive in welcoming this
interview with a registered Englishman was to get,
free of charge, an allopathic dose of 24-karat
English. I wanted to bask in the bright light of
an intellect that had no flickers in it and absorb
some of the infallibility that is so prevalent in these
parts.

We met. I steadied myself and said:—" I'm glad
to know you—that is, I am extremely pleased to
have the honour of making your acquaintance."

He looked at me with a kindly light in his steel blue eye, and after a short period of deliberation spoke as follows:—" Thanks."

" The international developments of recent years have been such as should properly engender a feeling of the warmest brotherhood between all branches of the Anglo-Saxon race," I said. " I don't think that any fair-minded American has it in for Great Britain—that is, it seems to me that all former resentment growing out of early conflicts between the two countries has given way to a spirit of tolerant understanding. Do you not agree with me? "

He hesitated for a moment, as if not desiring to commit himself by a hasty or impassioned reply, and then delivered himself as follows:—" Quite."

" It seems to me," I said, following the same line of thought, " that fair-minded people on both sides of the water are getting sore—that is, losing patience with the agitators who preach the old doctrine that our attitude toward Great Britain is necessarily one of enmity. We cannot forget that when the European Powers attempted to concert their influence against the United States at the outset of the late war with Spain you bluffed them out—that is, you induced them to relinquish their unfriendly intentions. Every thoughtful man in America is on to

12

" *Thanks* "

13

this fact—that is, he understands how important was the service you rendered us—and he is correspondingly grateful. The American people and the English people speak the same language, theoretically. Our interests are practically identical in all parts of the world—that is, we are trying to do everybody, and so are you. What I want to convey is that neither nation can properly work out its destiny except by co-operating with the other. Therefore any policy looking toward a severance of friendly relations is unworthy of consideration."

" Rot ! " said he.

" Just at present all Americans are profoundly grateful to the British public for its generous recognition of the sterling qualities of our beloved Executive," I continued. " Over in the States we think that ' Teddy ' is the goods—that is, the people of all sections have unbounded faith in him. We think he is on the level—that is, that his dominant policies are guided by the spirit of integrity. As a fair-minded Briton, who is keeping in touch with the affairs of the world, may I ask you your candid opinion of President Roosevelt? "

After a brief pause he spoke as follows:—
" Ripping ! "

" The impulse of friendliness on the part of the

14

English people seems to be more evident year by year," I continued. " It is now possible for Americans to get into nearly all the London hotels. You show your faith in our monetary system by accepting all the collateral we can bring over. No identification is necessary. Formerly the visiting American was asked to give references before he was separated from his income—that is, before one of your business institutions would enter into negotiations with him. Nowadays you see behind the chin whisker the beautiful trade mark of consanguinity. You say, ' Blood is thicker than water,' and you accept a five-dollar bill just the same as if it were an English sovereign worth four dollars and eighty-six cents."

" Jolly glad to get it," said he.

" Both countries have adopted the gospel of reciprocity," I said, warmed by this sudden burst of enthusiasm. " We send shiploads of tourists over here. You send shiploads of English actors to New York. The tourists go home as soon as they are broke—that is, as soon as their funds are exhausted. The English actors come home as soon as they are independently rich. Everybody is satisfied with the arrangement and the international bonds are further strengthened. Of course, some of the English actors blow up—that is, fail to meet with any great measure of financial success—when they get out as far as Omaha, but while they are mystifying the American public some of our tourists are going around London mystifying the British public. Doubtless you have seen some of these tourists? "

The distinguished person nodded his head in grave acquiescence and then said with some feeling:—
" Bounders! "

" In spite of these breaches of international faith the situation taken as a whole is one promising an indefinite continuation of cordial friendship between the Powers," I said. " I am darned glad that such is the case; ain't you? "

" Rather," he replied.

Then we parted.

It was really worth a long sea voyage to be permitted to get the English language at first hand; to revel in its unexpected sublimities, and gaze down new and awe-inspiring vistas of rhetorical splendour.

CHAPTER II

A LIFE ON THE OCEAN WAVE, WITH MODERN VARIATIONS

A MONTH before sailing I visited the floating skyscraper which was to bear us away. It was hitched to a dock in Hoboken, and it reminded me of a St. Bernard dog tied by a silken thread. It was the biggest skiff afloat, with an observatory on the roof and covered porches running all the way around. It was a very large boat.

After inspecting the boat and approving of it, I selected a room with southern exposure. Later on, when we sailed, the noble craft backed into the river and turned round before heading for the Old World, and I found myself on the north side of the ship, with nothing coming in at the porthole except a current of cold air direct from Labrador.

This room was on the starboard or port side of the ship—I forget which. After travelling nearly one million miles, more or less, by steamer, I am still unable to tell which is starboard and which is port. I can tell time by the ship's bell if you let me use a

17

pencil, but " starboard " means nothing to me. In
order to make it clear to the reader, I will say that
the room was on the " haw " side of the boat. I
thought I was getting the " gee " side as the vessel
lay at the dock, but I forgot that it had to turn

I complained to one of the officers

around in order to start for Europe, and I found
myself " haw." I complained to one of the officers
and said that I had engaged a stateroom with
southern exposure. He said they couldn't back up

18

all the way across the Atlantic just to give me the sunny side of the boat. This closed the incident. He did explain, however, that if I remained in the ship and went back with them I would have southern exposure all the way home.

Our ship was the latest thing out. To say that it was about seven hundred feet long and nearly sixty feet beam and 42,000 tons displacement does not give a graphic idea of its huge proportions. A New Yorker might understand if told that this ship, stood on end, would be about as tall as two Flatiron buildings spliced end to end.

Out in Indiana this comparison was unavailing, as few of the residents have seen the Flatiron Building and only a small percentage of them have any desire to see it. So when a Hoosier acquaintance asked me something about the ship I led him out into Main Street and told him that it would reach from the railroad to the Presbyterian church. He looked down street at the depot and then he looked up street at the distant Presbyterian church, and then he looked at me and walked away. Every statement that I make in my native town is received with doubt. People have mistrusted me ever since I came home years ago and announced that I was working.

Evidently he repeated what I had said, for in a

few minutes another resident came up and casually asked me something about the ship and wanted to know how long she was. I repeated the Presbyterian church story. He merely remarked "I thought ' Bill ' was lyin' to me," and then went his way.

It is hard to live down a carefully acquired reputation, and therefore the statement as to the length of the vessel was regarded as a specimen outburst of native humour. When I went on to say that the boat would have on board three times as many people as there were in our whole town, that she had seven decks, superimposed like the layers of a jelly cake, that elevators carried passengers from one deck to another, that a daily newspaper was printed on board, and that a brass band gave concerts every day, to say nothing of the telephone exchange and the free bureau of information, then all doubt was dispelled and my local standing as a dealer in morbid fiction was largely fortified.

The chief wonder of our new liner (for all of us had a proprietary interest the moment we came aboard) was the system of elevators. Just think of it! Elevators gliding up and down between decks the same as in a modern office building. Very few passengers used the elevators, but it gave us something to talk about on board ship and it would give us something to blow about after we had returned home.

Outside of the cage stood a young German with a blonde pompadour and a jacket that came just below his shoulder blades. He was so clean he looked as if he had been scrubbed with soap and then rubbed with holystone. Every German menial on board seemed to have two guiding ambitions in life. One was to keep himself immaculate and the other was to grow a U-shaped moustache, the same as the one worn by the Kaiser.

The boy in charge of the elevator would plead with people to get in and ride. Usually, unless he waylaid them, they would forget all about the new improvement and would run up and down stairs in the old-fashioned manner instituted by Noah and imitated by Christopher Columbus.

This boy leads a checkered career on each voyage. When he departs from New York he is the elevator boy. As the vessel approaches Plymouth, England, he becomes the lift attendant. At Cherbourg he is transformed into a *garçon d'ascenseur,* and as the ship draws near Hamburg he is the *Aufzugsbehueter,* which is an awful thing to call a mere child.

Goodness only knows what will be the ultimate result of present competition between ocean liners. As our boat was quite new and extravagantly up-to-date, perhaps some information concerning it will be of interest, even to those old and hardened travellers who have been across so often that they no longer set down the run of the ship and have ceased sending pictorial post-cards to their friends at home.

In the first place, a telephone in every room, connected with a central station. The passenger never uses it, because when he is a thousand miles from shore there is no one to be called up, and if he needs the steward he pushes a button. But it is there—a real German telephone, shaped like a broken pretzel, and anyone who has a telephone in his room feels that he is getting something for his money.

After two or three lessons any American can use a foreign telephone. All he has to learn is which end to put to his ear and how to keep two or three springs pressed down all the time he is talking. In America he takes down the receiver and talks into the 'phone. Elsewhere he takes the entire telephone down from a rack and holds it the same as a slide trombone.

In some of the cabins were electric hair curlers. A Cleveland man who wished to call up the adjoining cabin on the 'phone, just to see if the thing would

Holds it the same as a slide trombone

work, put the hair curler to his ear and began
talking into the dynamo. There was no response, so
he pushed a button and nearly ruined his left ear.
It was a natural mistake. In Europe, anything
attached to the wall is liable to be a telephone.

On the whole, I think our telephone system is superior to that of any foreign cities. Our telephone
girls have larger vocabularies, for one thing. In
England the " hello " is never used. When an Englishman gathers up the ponderous contrivance and
fits it against his head he asks:—" Are you there? "
If the other man answers " No," that stops the
whole conversation.

Travellers throughout the world should rise up
and unite in a vote of thanks to whoever it was that
abolished the upper berth in the newer boats. Maho-
met's coffin suspended in mid air must have been a
cheery and satisfactory bunk compared with the ordinary upper berth. Only a trained athlete can climb
into one of them. The woodwork that you embrace
and rub your legs against as you struggle upward
is very cold. When you fall into the clammy sheets
you are only about six inches from the ceiling. In the
early morning the sailors scour the deck just overhead and you feel as if you were getting a shampoo.
The aërial sarcophagus is built deep, like a trough,

so that the prisoner cannot roll out during the night. It is narrow, and the man who is addicted to the habit of "spraddling" feels as if he were tied hand and foot.

In nearly all of the staterooms of the new boat there were no upper berths, and the lower ones were wide and springy—they were almost beds, and a bed on board ship is something that for years has been reserved as the special luxury of the million- aire.

I like the democracy of a shipboard community. You take the most staid and awe-inspiring notable in the world, bundle him in a damp storm-coat and pull a baggy travelling cap down over his ears and there is none so humble as to do him reverence. One passenger may say to another as this great man teeters along the deck, squinting against the wind: " Do you know who that man is? "

" No, who is it? "

" That's William Bilker, the millionaire philan- thropist. He owns nearly all the coke ovens in the world—has built seven theological seminaries. He's going to Europe to escape a Congressional investigation."

That is the end of it so far as any flattering attentions to Mr. Bilker are concerned. If he goes

25

in the smoking-room some beardless youth will invite him to sit in a game of poker. His confidential friend at the table may be a Montana miner, a Chicago real estate agent or a Kentucky horseman. He may hold himself aloof from the betting crowd and discourage those who would talk with him on deck, but he cannot by any possibility be a man of importance. Compared with the captain, for instance, he is a worm. And the captain draws probably $2500 a year. It must be a lot of fun to stay on board ship all the time. Otherwise the ocean liner could not get so many high class and capable men to work for practically nothing.

On the open sea a baby is much more interesting than a railway president and juveniles in general are a mighty welcome addition to the passenger list. If a child in the house is a wellspring of pleasure, then a child on a boat is nothing less than a waterspout. The sea air, with its cool vapours of salt and iodine, may lull the adult into one continuous and lazy doze, but it is an invigorant to the offspring. We had on board children from Buffalo, Chicago, Jamestown, Poughkeepsie, Worcester, Philadelphia, and other points. These children traded names before the steamer got away from the dock, and as we went down the bay under a bright sunshine they were so full of emotion that they ran madly around the upper decks, shrieking at every step. Nine full laps on the upper deck make a mile, and one man gave the opinion that the children travelled one hundred miles that first afternoon. This was probably an exaggeration.

The older people lay at full length in steamer chairs and drowsed like so many hibernating bears. That is, they slept when they were not eating. The boat was one of a German line, and on a German boat the passenger's first duty is to gorge. In the smoking-room the last night out there was a dispute as to the number of meals, whole or partial, served every day. One man counted up and made it nine. Another, who was trying to slander the company, made the number as low as five. A count was taken and the following schedule was declared to be accurate and official:

6 a. m.—Coffee and rolls in the dining room.

8 to 10 a. m.—Breakfast in the dining room.

11 a. m.—Sandwiches and bouillon on deck.

12:35 p. m.—Luncheon.

4 p. m.—Cakes and lemonade on deck.

6 p. m.—Dinner.

9 p. m.—Supper (cold) in dining room.

10 to 11:30 p. m.—Sandwiches (Swiss cheese,

caviar, tongue, beef, cervelat wurst, etc.) in the smoking-room.

It will be noted that anyone using ordinary diligence is enabled to stay the pangs of hunger at least eight times a day. But the company in order to cover all emergencies, has made the humane provision that articles of food may be obtained at any hour, either in the smoking room or dining room, or by giving the order to a steward. It is said that geese being fattened for the market or encouraged to develop the liver are tied to the ground so that they cannot take any harmful exercise, and large quantities of rich food are then pushed into them by means of a stick. Anyone who has spent a lazy week on a German steamer can sympathise with the geese.

Of course we had wireless messages to give us an occasional throb of excitement. Wireless telegraphy, by the way, is more or less of an irritant to the traveller. The man with stocks purchased and lawsuits pending, and all sorts of deals under way, knows that he can be reached (probably) in some sort of a zig-zag manner by wireless telegraphy, no matter where he may be on the wide ocean, and so, most of the time, he is standing around on one foot waiting for bad news. On shore he doesn't fret so much about possible calamities, but as soon as he gets away from Sandy Hook he begins to draw mental pictures of the mistakes being made by lunk-headed subordinates, and then he hangs around the Marconi station up on the sun deck, waiting for his most horrible fears to be confirmed.

In 1895, during my first voyage to Europe, I wrote the following in one of my letters, intending it as a mild pleasantry:

" Some day, perhaps, there will be invented a device by which ocean steamers may tap the Atlantic cable for news bulletins and stock quotations, or else receive them by special transmission through the water, and then the last refuge will be denied the business slave who is attempting to get away from his work."

And to think that ten years later the miracle of shooting a message through an open window and across five hundred miles of nothing but atmosphere has become a tame and every-day occurrence!

On the steamer I met an old friend—Mr. Peasley, of Iowa. We first collided in Europe in 1895, when both of us were over for the first time and were groping our way about the Continent and pretending to enjoy ourselves. About the time I first encountered Mr. Peasley he had an experience which, in all probability, is without parallel in human history. Some people to whom I have told the story frankly disbelieved it, but then they did not know Mr. Peasley. It is all very true, and it happened as follows:—

Mr. Peasley had been in Rotterdam for two days, and after galloping madly through churches, galleries, and museums for eight hours a day he said that he had seen enough Dutch art to last him a million years, at a very conservative estimate, so he started for Brussels. He asked the proprietor of the hotel at Rotterdam for the name of a good hotel in Brussels and the proprietor told him to go to the Hotel Victoria. He said it was a first-class establishment and was run by his brother-in-law. Every hotel keeper in Europe has a brother-in-law running a hotel in some other town.

Mr. Peasley was loaded into a train by watchful attendants, and as there were no Englishmen in the compartment he succeeded in getting a good seat right by the window and did not have to ride backward. Very soon he became immersed in one of the six best sellers. He read on and on, chapter after chapter, not heeding the flight of time, until the train rolled into a cavernous train shed and was attacked by the usual energetic mob of porters and hotel runners. Mr. Peasley looked out and saw that they had arrived at another large city. On the other side of the platform was a large and beautiful 'bus marked " Hotel Victoria." Mr. Peasley shrieked for a porter and began dumping Gladstone bags, steamer rugs, cameras, and other impedimenta out through the window. The man from the Victoria put these on top of the 'bus and in a few minutes Mr. Peasley was riding through the tidy thoroughfares and throwing mental bouquets at the street-cleaning department.

When he arrived at the Victoria he was met by the proprietor, who wore the frock coat and whiskers which are the world-wide insignia of hospitality.

" Your brother-in-law in Rotterdam told me to come here and put up with you," explained Mr. Peasley. " He said you were running a first-class place, which means, I s'pose, first class for this country. If you fellows over here would put in steam heat and bathrooms and electric lights and then give us something to eat in the bargain your hotels wouldn't be so bad. I admire the stationery in your writing rooms, and the regalia worn by your waiters is certainly all right, but that's about all I can say for you."

The proprietor smiled and bowed and said he hoped his brother-in-law in Rotterdam was in good

health and enjoying prosperity, and Mr. Peasley said
that he, personally, had left with the brother-in-law
enough money to run the hotel for another six
months.

After Mr. Peasley had been conducted to his room
he dug up his Baedeker and very carefully read the
introduction to Brussels. Then he studied the map
for a little while. He believed in getting a good
general idea of the lay of things before he tackled
a new town. He marked on the map a few of the show
places which seemed worth while, and then he sallied
out, waving aside the smirking guide who attempted
to fawn upon him as he paused at the main entrance.
Mr. Peasley would have nothing to do with guides.
He always said that the man who had to be led
around by the halter would do better to stay right
at home.

It was a very busy afternoon for Mr. Peasley.
At first he had some difficulty in finding the places
that were marked in red spots on the map. This was
because he had been holding the map upside down.
By turning the map the other way and making due
allowance for the inaccuracies to be expected in a
book written by ignorant foreigners, the whole
ground plan of the city straightened itself out, and
he boldly went his way. He visited an old cathedral

and two art galleries, reading long and scholarly comments on the more celebrated masterpieces. Some of the paintings were not properly labelled, but he knew that slipshod methods prevailed in Europe—that a civilisation which is on the downhill and about to play out cannot be expected to breed a business-like accuracy. He wrote marginal corrections in his guide book and doctored up the map a little, several streets having been omitted, and returned to the hotel at dusk feeling very well repaid. From the beginning of his tour he had maintained that when a man goes out and gets information or impressions of his own unaided efforts he gets something that will abide with him and become a part of his intellectual and artistic fibre. That which is ladled into him by a verbose guide soon evaporates or oozes away.

At the *table d'hôte* Mr. Peasley had the good fortune to be seated next to an Englishman, to whom he addressed himself. The Englishman was not very communicative, but Mr. Peasley persevered. It was his theory that when one is travelling and meets a fellow Caucasian who is shy or reticent or suspicious the thing to do is to keep on talking to him until he feels quite at ease and the *entente cordiale* is fully established. So Mr. Peasley told the Englishman all

about Iowa and said that it was " God's country."
The Englishman fully agreed with him—that is, if
silence gives consent. There was a lull in the conversation and Mr. Peasley, seeking to give it a new
turn, said to his neighbour, " I like this town best of
any I've seen. Is this your first visit to Brussels? "

" I have never been to Brussels," replied the Englishman.

" That is, never until this time," suggested Mr.
Peasley. " I'm in the same boat. Just landed here
to-day. I've heard of it before, on account of the
carpet coming from here, and of course everybody
knows about Brussels sprouts, but I had no idea
it was such a big place. It's bigger than Rock Island
and Davenport put together."

The Englishman began to move away, at the same
time regarding the cheerful Peasley with solemn
wonderment. Then he said :—

" My dear sir, I am quite unable to follow you.
Where do you think you are? "

" Brussels—it's in Belgium—capital, same as Des
Moines in Iowa."

" My good man, you are not in Brussels. You are
in Antwerp."

" Antwerp ! "

" Certainly."

" Why, I've been all over town to-day, with a guide book, and——" He paused and a horrible suspicion settled upon him. Arising from the table he rushed to the outer office and confronted the manager.

" What's the name of this town I'm in? " he demanded.

" Antwerp," replied the astonished manager.

Mr. Peasley leaned against the wall and gasped. " Well, I'll be ——! " he began, and then language failed him.

" You said you had a brother-in-law in Rotterdam," he said, when he recovered his voice.

" That is quite true."

" And the Victoria Hotel—is there one in Brussels and another in Antwerp? "

" There is a Victoria Hotel in every city in the whole world. The Victoria Hotel is universal—the same as Scotch whiskey."

" And I am now in Antwerp? "

" Most assuredly."

Mr. Peasley went to his room. He did not dare to return to face the Englishman. Next day he proceeded to Brussels and found that he could work from the same guide book just as successfully as he had in Antwerp.

When I met him on the steamer he said that during all of his travels since 1895 he never had duplicated the remarkable experience at Antwerp. As soon as he alights from a train he goes right up to someone and asks the name of the town.

CHAPTER III

WITH MR. PEASLEY IN DARKEST LONDON

WE did not expect to have Mr. Peasley with us in London. He planned to hurry on to Paris, but he has been waiting here for his trunk to catch up with him. The story of the trunk will come later.

As we steamed into Plymouth Harbour on a damp and overcast Sabbath morning, Mr. Peasley stood on the topmost deck and gave encouraging information to a man from central Illinois who was on his first trip abroad. Mr. Peasley had been over for six weeks in 1895, and that gave him license to do the " old traveller " specialty.

In beginning a story he would say, " I remember once I was crossing on the *Umbria*," or possibly, " That reminds me of a funny thing I once saw in Munich." He did not practise to deceive, and yet he gave strangers the impression that he had crossed on the *Umbria* possibly twelve or fourteen times and had spent years in Munich.

The Illinois man looked up to Mr. Peasley as a

modern Marco Polo, and Mr. Peasley proceeded to
unbend to him.

"A few years ago Americans were very unpopular in England," said Mr. Peasley. "Every one of
them was supposed to have either a dynamite bomb
or a bunch of mining stock in his pocket. All that
is changed now—all changed. As we come up to
the dock in Plymouth you will notice just beyond the
station a large triumphal arch of evergreen bearing
the words, 'Welcome, Americans!' Possibly the band
will not be out this morning, because it is Sunday
and the weather is threatening, but the Reception
Committee will be on hand. If we can take time before starting for London no doubt a committee from
the Commercial Club will haul us around in open
carriages to visit the public buildings and breweries
and other points of interest. And you'll find that
your money is counterfeit out here. No use talkin',
we're all one people—just like brothers. Wait till
you get to London. You'll think you're right back
among your friends in Decatur."

It was too early in the morning for the Reception
Committee, but there was a policeman—one solitary,
water-logged, sad-eyed policeman—waiting grew-
somely on the dock as the tender came alongside. He
stood by the gangplank and scrutinised us carefully

as we filed ashore. The Illinois man looked about for the triumphal arch, but could not find it. Mr. Peasley explained that they had taken it in on account of the rain.

While the passengers were kept herded into a rather gloomy waiting room, the trunks and larger baggage were brought ashore and sorted out according to the alphabetical labels in an adjoining room to await the customs examination. When the doors opened there was a rush somewhat like the opening of an Oklahoma reservation. In ten minutes the trunks had been passed and were being trundled out to the special train. Above the babel of voices and the rattle of wheels arose the sounds of lamentation and modified cuss words. Mr. Peasley could not find his trunk. It was not with the baggage marked " P." It was not in the boneyard, or the discard, or whatever they call the heap of unmarked stuff piled up at one end of the room. It was not anywhere.

The other passengers, intent upon their private troubles, pawed over their possessions and handed out shillings right and left and followed the line of trucks out to the " luggage vans," and Mr. Peasley was left alone, still demanding his trunk. The station agent and many porters ran hither and thither, looking into all sorts of impossible places, while the locomotive bell rang warningly, and the guard begged Mr. Peasley to get aboard if he wished to go to London. Mr. Peasley took off his hat and leaned his head back and howled for his trunk. The train

And howled for his trunk

started and Mr. Peasley, after momentary inde-cision, made a running leap into our midst. There were six of us in a small padded cell, and five of the six listened for the next fifteen minutes to a most picturesque and impassioned harangue on the subject of the general inefficiency of German steamships and English railways.

"Evidently the trunk was not sent ashore," someone suggested to Mr. Peasley. "If the trunk did not come ashore you could not reasonably expect the station officials to find it and put it aboard the train."

"But why didn't it come ashore?" demanded Mr. Peasley. "Everyone on the boat knew that I was going to get off at Plymouth. It was talked about all the way over. Other people got their trunks, didn't they? Have you heard of any German being shy a trunk? Has anybody else lost anything? No; they went over the passenger list and said, ' If we must hold out a trunk on anyone, let's hold it out on Peasley—old good thing Peasley."

"Are you sure it was put on board at Hoboken?" he was asked.

"Sure thing. I checked it myself, or, rather, I got a fellow that couldn't speak any English to check it for me. Then I saw it lowered into the cellar, or the subway, or whatever they call it."

"Did you get a receipt for it?"

"You bet I did, and right here she is."

He brought out a congested card case and fum-

Let's hold it out on Peasley

42

bled over a lot of papers, and finally unfolded a receipt about the size of a one-sheet poster. On top was a number and beneath it said in red letters at least two inches tall, " This baggage has been checked to Hamburg."

We called Mr. Peasley's attention to the reading matter, but he said it was a mistake, because he had been intending all the time to get off at Plymouth.

" Nevertheless, your trunk has gone to Hamburg."

" Where is Hamburg? "

" In Germany. The Teuton who checked your baggage could not by any effort of the imagination conceive the possibility of a person starting for anywhere except Hamburg. In two days your trunk will be lying on a dock in Germany."

" Well, there's one consolation," observed Mr. Peasley; " the clothes in that trunk won't fit any German."

When he arrived in London he began wiring for his trunk in several languages. After two days came a message couched in Volapuk or some other hybrid combination, which led him to believe that his property had been started for London.

Mr. Peasley spent a week in the world's metropolis

with no clothes except a knockabout travelling outfit and what he called his " Tuxedo," although, over here they say " dinner jacket." In Chicago or Omaha Mr. Peasley could have got along for a week without any embarrassment to himself or others. Even in New York the " Tuxedo " outfit would have carried him through, for it is regarded as a passable apology for evening dress, provided the wearer wishes to advertise himself as a lonesome " stag." But in London there is no compromise. In every hotel lobby or dining-room, every restaurant, theatre or music hall, after the coagulated fog of the daytime settles into the opaque gloom of night, there is but one style of dress for any mortal who does not wish to publicly pose as a barbarian. The man who affects a " Tuxedo " might as well wear a sweater. In fact it would be better for him if he did wear a sweater, for then people would understand that he was making no effort to dress; but when he puts on a bobtail he conveys the impression that he is trying to be correct and doesn't understand the rules.

An Englishman begins to blossom about half-past seven P. M. The men seen in the streets during the day seem a pretty dingy lot compared with a well-dressed stream along Fifth Avenue. Many of the tall hats bear a faithful resemblance to fur caps. The trousers bag and the coat collars are bunched in the rear and all the shoes seem about two sizes too large. Occasionally you see a man on his way to a train and he wears a shapeless bag of a garment made of some loosely woven material that looks like gunny-sack, with a cap that resembles nothing so much as

" Dressed down " and " Dressed up "

a welsh rabbit that has " spread." To complete the picture, he carries a horse blanket. He thinks it is a rug, but it isn't. It is a horse blanket.

If the Englishman dressed for travel is the most

sloppy of all civilised beings, so the Englishman in
his night regalia is the most correct and irreproach-
able of mortals. He can wear evening clothes without being conscious of the fact that he is " dressed
up." The trouble with the ordinary American who
owns an open-faced suit is that he wears it only
about once a month. For two days before assuming
the splendour of full dress he broods over the approaching ordeal. As the fateful night draws near
he counts up his studs and investigates the " white
vest " situation. In the deep solitude of his room
he mournfully climbs into the camphor-laden garments, and when he is ready to venture forth, a tall
collar choking him above, the glassy shoes pinching
him below, he is just as much at ease as he would be
in a full suit of armour, with casque and visor.

However, all this is off the subject. Here was Mr.
Peasley in London, desirous of " cutting a wide
gash," as he very prettily termed it, plenty of good
money from Iowa burning in his pocket, and he could
not get out and " associate " because of a mere defi-
ciency in clothing.

At the first-class theatres his " bowler " hat condemned him and he was sent into the gallery. When
he walked into a restaurant the head waiter would
give him one quick and searching glance and then

put him off in some corner, behind a palm. Even in the music halls the surrounding "Johnnies" regarded him with wonder as another specimen of the eccentric Yankee.

We suggested to Mr. Peasley that he wear a

His bowler hat condemned him

placard reading "I have some clothes, but my trunk is in Hamburg." He said that as soon as his swell duds arrived he was going to put them on and revisit all of the places at which he had been humiliated and turned down, just to let the flunkeys know that they had been mistaken.

Mr. Peasley was greatly rejoiced to learn one day that he could attend a football game without wearing a special uniform. So he went out to see a non-brutal game played according to the Association rules. The gentle pastime known as football in America is a modification and overdevelopment of the Rugby game as played in Great Britain. The Association, or " Soccer " game, which is now being introduced in the United States as a counter-irritant for the old-fashioned form of manslaughter, is by far the more popular in England. The Rugby Association is waning in popularity, not because of any outcry against the character of the play or any talk of " brutality," but because the British public has a more abiding fondness for the Association game.

In America we think we are football crazy because we have a few big college games during October and November of each year. In Great Britain the football habit is something that abides, the same as the tea habit.

We are hysterical for about a month and then we forget the game unless we belong to the minority that is trying to debrutalise it and reduce the death rate.

MR. PEASLEY IN DARKEST LONDON

Here it was, February in London, and on the first Saturday after our arrival forty-five Association games and thirty-eight Rugby games were reported in the London papers. At sixteen of the principal Association games the total attendance was over two hundred and fifty thousand and the actual receipts at these same games amounted to about $45,000. There were two games at each of which the attendance was over thirty thousand, with the receipts exceeding $5,000. A very conservative estimate of the total attendance at the games played on this Saturday would be five hundred thousand. In other words, on one Saturday afternoon in February the attendance at football games was equal to the total attendance at all of the big college games during an entire season in the United States. No wonder that the English newspapers are beginning to ask editorially " Is football a curse? " There is no clamour regarding the roughness of the game, but it is said to cost too much money and to take up too much time for the benefits derived.

The game to which Mr. Peasley conducted us was played in rather inclement weather—that is, inclement London weather—which means that it was the most terrible day that the imagination can picture—a dark, chilly, drippy day, with frequent downpours.

It has been said that one cannot obtain icewater in London. This is a mistake. We obtained it by the hogshead.

In spite of the fact that the weather was bad beyond description, seventeen thousand spectators attended the game and saw it through to a watery finish.

Mr. Peasley looked on and was much disappointed. He said they used too many players and the number of fatalities was not at all in keeping with the advertised importance of the game. It was a huge crowd, but the prevailing spirit of solemnity worried Mr. Peasley. He spoke to a native standing alongside of him and asked:—"What's the matter with you folks over here? Don't you know how to back up a team? Where are all of your flags and ribbons, your tally-hos and tin horns? Is this a football game or a funeral?"

"Why should one wear ribbons at a football game?" asked the Englishman.

"Might as well put a little ginger into the exercises," suggested Mr. Peasley. "Do you sing during the game?"

"Heavens, no. Sing? Why should one sing during a football game? In what manner is vocal music related to an outdoor pastime of this character?"

"You ought to go to a game in Iowa City. We sing till we're black in the face—all about ' Eat 'em up, boys,' 'Kill 'em in their tracks,' and ' Buck through the line.' What's the use of coming to a game if you stand around all afternoon and don't take part? Have you got any yells? "

" What are those? "

" Can you beat that? " asked Mr. Peasley, turning to us. " A football game without any yells! "

The game started. By straining our eyes we could make out through the deep gloom some thirty energetic young men, very lightly clad, splashing about in all directions, and kicking in all sorts of aimless directions. Mr. Peasley said it was a mighty poor excuse for football. No one was knocked out; there was no bucking the line; there didn't even seem to be a doctor in evidence. We could not follow the fine points of the contest. Evidently some good plays were being made, for occasionally a low, growling sound—a concerted murmur—would arise from the multitude banked along the side lines.

" What is the meaning of that sound they are making? " asked Mr. Peasley, turning to the native standing alongside of him.

" They are cheering," was the reply.

" They are what? "

51

" Cheering."

" Great Scott! Do you call that cheering? At home, when we want to encourage the boys we get up on our hind legs and make a noise that you can hear in the next township. We put cracks in the azure dome. Cheering! Why, a game of croquet in the court house yard is eight times as thrilling as this thing. Look at those fellows juggling the ball with their feet. Why doesn't somebody pick it up and butt through that crowd and start a little rough work? "

The native gave Mr. Peasley one hopeless look and moved away.

We could not blame our companion for being disappointed over the cheering. An English cheer is not the ear-splitting demoniacal shriek, such as an American patriot lets out when he hears from another batch of precincts.

The English cheer is simply a loud grunt, or a sort of guttural " Hey! hey!" or " Hurray!"

When an English crowd cheers the sound is similar to that made by a Roman mob in the wings of a theatre.

After having once heard the " cheering " one can understand the meaning of a passage in the Parliamentary report, reading about as follows: " The gentleman hoped the house would not act with haste. (Cheers). He still had confidence in the committee (cheers), but would advise a careful consideration (cheers), etc."

It might be supposed from such a report that Parliament was one continuous " rough house," but we looked in one day and it is more like a cross between a Presbyterian synod and bee-keepers' convention.

About four o'clock we saw a large section of the football crowd moving over toward a booth at one end of the grounds. Mr. Peasley hurried after them, thinking that possibly someone had started a fight on the side and that his love of excitement might be gratified after all. Presently he returned in a state of deep disgust.

" Do you know why all those folks are flockin' over there? " he asked. " Goin' after their tea. Tea! Turnin' their backs on a football game to go and get a cup of tea! Why, that tea thing over there is worse than the liquor habit. Do you know, when the final judgment day comes and Gabriel blows his horn and all of humanity is bunched up, waitin' for the sheep to be cut out from the goats and put into a separate corral, some Englishman will look at his watch and discover that it's five o'clock and then the whole British nation will turn its back on the proceedings and go off looking for tea."

After we had stood in the rain for about an hour someone told Mr. Peasley that one team or the other had won by three goals to nothing, and we followed the moist throng out through the big gates.

" Come with me," said Mr. Peasley, " and I will take you to the only dry place in London."

So we descended to the " tuppenny tube."

CHAPTER IV

HOW IT FEELS TO GET INTO LONDON AND THEN BE ENGULFED.

ONE good thing about London is that, in spite of its enormous size, you are there when you arrive. Take Chicago, by way of contrast. If you arrive in Chicago along about the middle of the afternoon you may be at the station by night.

The stranger heading into Chicago looks out of the window at a country station and sees a policeman standing on the platform. Beyond is a sign indicating that the wagon road winding away toward the sunset is 287th street, or thereabouts.

" We are now in Chicago," says someone who has been over che road before.

The traveller, surprised to learn that he has arrived at his destination, puts his magazine and travelling cap into the valise, shakes out his overcoat, calls on the porter to come and brush him, and then sits on the end of the seat waiting for the brakeman to announce the terminal station. After a half-hour of intermittent suburbs and glorious sweeps of virgin prairie he begins to think that there is some mistake, so he opens his valise and takes out the magazine and reads another story.

Suddenly he looks out of the window and notices that the train has entered the crowded city. He puts on his overcoat, picks up his valise and stands in the aisle, so as to be ready to step right off as soon as the train stops.

The train passes street after street and rattles through grimy yards and past towering elevators, and in ten minutes the traveller tires of standing and goes back to his seat. The porter comes and brushes him again, and he looks out at several viaducts leading over to a skyline of factories and breweries, and begins to see the masts of ships poking up in the most unexpected places. At last, when he has looked at what seems to be one hundred miles of architectural hash floating in smoke and has begun to doubt that there is a terminal station, he hears the welcome call, " Shuh-kawgo! "

When you are London bound the train leaves the green country (for the country is green, even in February), dashes into a region of closely built streets, and you look out from the elevated train across an endless expanse of chimney-pots. Two or three stations, plated with enameled advertising signs, buzz past. The pall of smoky fog becomes heavier and the streets more crowded. Next, the train has come to a grinding stop under a huge vaulted roof. The noise of the wheels give way to the roar of London town.

You step down and out and fall into the arms of a porter who wishes to carry your " bags." You are in the midst of parallel tracks and shifting trains. Beyond the platform is a scramble of cabs. The sounds of the busy station are joined into a deafening monotone. You shout into the ear of your travelling companion to get a " four-wheeler " while you watch the trunks.

He struggles away to hail a four-wheeler. You push your way with the others down toward the front of the train to where the baggage is being thrown out on the platform. You seize a porter and engage him to attend to the handling of the trunks. As you point them out he loads them onto a truck. Your companion arrives in a wild-eyed search for you.

" I've got a four-wheeler," he gasps. " All the baggage here? "

" Yes, yes, yes."

Everybody is excited and hopping about, put

into a state of hysteria by the horrible hubbub and confusion.

" It's number 48."

The porter handling the truck leads the way to the cab platform and howls " Forty-ite! Forty-ite! "

" 'Ere you are," shouts forty-eight, who is wedged in behind two hansoms.

By some miracle of driving he gets over or under or past the hansoms and comes to the platform. The steamer trunks are thrown on top and the porter, accepting the shilling with a " 'k you, sir," slams the door behind you.

Then you can hear your driver overhead managing his way out of the blockade.

" Pull a bit forward, cahn't you? " he shouts. Then to someone else, " 'Urry up, 'urry up, cahn't you? "

You are in a tangle of wheels and lamps, but you get out of it in some way, and then the rubber tires roll easily along the spattering pavement of a street which seems heavenly quietude.

This is the time to lean back and try to realise that you are in London. The town may be common and time-worn to those people going in and out of the shops, but to you it is a storehouse of novelties, a library of things to be learned, a museum of the landmarks of history.

We could read the names on the windows, and they were good homely Anglo-Saxon names. We didn't have to get out of the four-wheeler and go into the shops to convince ourselves that Messrs. Brown, Jones, Simpson, Perkins, Jackson, Smith, Thompson, Williams, and the others were serious men of deferential habits, who spoke in hollow whispers of the king, drank tea at intervals and loved a pipe of tobacco in the garden of a Sunday morning.

Some people come to London to see the Abbey and the Tower, but I fear that our trusty little band came to see the shop windows and the crowds in the streets.

May the weak and imitative traveller resist the temptation to say that Fleet street is full of publishing houses, that the British museum deserves many visits, that the Cheshire Cheese is one of the ancient taverns, that the new monument in front of the Courts of Law marks the site of old Temple Bar, that the chapel of King Henry VII. is a superb example of its own style of decoration, and that one is well repaid for a trip to Hampton Court. Why seek to corroborate the testimony of so many letter-writers?

Besides, London does not consist of towers, abbeys, and museums. These are the remote and infrequent things. After you have left London and try to call back the huge and restless picture to your mind, the show places stand dimly in the background. The London which impressed you and made you feel your own littleness and weakness was an endless swarm of people going and coming, eddying off into dark courts, streaming toward you along sudden tributaries, whirling in pools at the open places, such as Piccadilly Circus and Trafalgar Square. Thousands of hansom cabs dashed in and out of the street traffic, and the rattling omnibuses moved along every street in a broken row, and no matter how long you remained in London you never saw the end of that row.

You go out in London in the morning, and if you have no set programme to hamper you, you make your way to one of those great chutes along which the herds of humanity are forever driven.

If you follow the guide-book it will lead you to a chair in which a king sat 300 years ago. If you can get up an emotion by straining hard enough and find a real pleasure in looking at the moth-eaten chair, then you should follow the guide-book. If not, escape from the place and go to the street. The men and women you find there will interest you. They are on deck. The chair is a dead splinter of his-

tory. All the people in the street are the embodi-
ment of that history. For purposes of actual observation I would rather encounter a live cabman than
the intangible, atmospheric suggestion of Queen
Elizabeth.

After you have been in London once you understand why your friends who have visited it before
were never able to tell you about it so that you
could understand. It is too big to be put under one
focus. The traveller takes home only a few idiotic
details of his stay. He says that he had to pay for
his programme at the theatre, and that he couldn't
get ice at some of the restaurants.

"But tell us about London," says the insistent
friend who has constructed a London of his own out
of a thousand impressions gathered from books and
magazines. Then the traveller says that London is
large, he doesn't remember how many millions, and
very busy, and there wasn't as much fog as he had
expected, and as for the people they were not so
much different from Americans, although you never
had any difficulty in identifying an American in
London. The traveller's friends listen in disappoint-
ment and agree that he got very little out of his
trip, and that when *they* go to London *they* will
come back and tell people the straight of it.

As a matter of fact, London is principally a sense of dizziness. This dizziness comes of trying to keep an intent gaze on too many human performances. The mind is in a blur. The impressions come with rolling swiftness. There is no room for them. The traveller overflows with them. They spill behind him. You could track an American all around London by the trail of excess information which he drops in his pathway.

Of course, I have kept a journal, but that doesn't help much. It simply says that we went out each day and then came back to the hotel for dinner. There was not much chance for personal experiences, because in London you are not a person. You are simply a drop of water in a sea, and any molecular disturbances which may concern you are of small moment compared to the general splash.

CHAPTER V

AS TO THE IMPORTANCE OF THE PASS-
PORT AND THE HANDY LITTLE
CABLE CODE

ADVICE to those following along behind. Stock up on heavy flannels and do not bother about a passport.

Before we became old and hardened travellers we were led to believe that any American who appeared at a frontier without a passport would be hurried to a dungeon or else marched in the snow all the way to Siberia.

When I first visited the eastern hemisphere (I *do* love to recall the fact that I have been over here before), our little company of travellers prepared for European experiences by reading a small hand-book of advice. The topics were arranged alpha-betically, and the specific information set out under each heading was more valuable and impressive at the beginning of the trip than it was after we had come home and read it in the cold light of experience. We paid particular heed to the following:

" PASSPORTS—Every American travelling in Europe should carry a passport. At many frontiers a passport, properly ' vised,' must be shown before the traveller will be allowed to enter the country. A passport is always valuable as an identification when money is to be drawn on a letter of credit. Very often it will secure for the bearer admission to palaces, galleries and other show places which are closed to the general public. It is the most ready answer to any police inquiry, and will serve as a letter of introduction to all consular offices."

We read the foregoing and sent for passports before we bought our steamship tickets.

I have been a notary public; I have graduated from a highschool; I have taken out accident insurance, and once, in a careless moment, I purchased one thousand shares of mining stock. In each instance I received a work of art on parchment—something bold and black and Gothic, garnished with gold seals and curly-cues. But for splendour of composition and majesty of design, the passport makes all other important documents seem pale and pointless. There is an American eagle at the top, with his trousers turned up, and beneath is a bold pronouncement to the world in general that the bearer is an American citizen, entitled to everything that he can afford to buy. No man can read his own passport without being more or less stuck on himself. I never had a chance to use the one given to me years ago, but I still keep it and read it once in a while to bolster up my self-respect.

When we first landed at Liverpool each man had his passport in his inside coat pocket within easy reach, so that in case of an insult or an impertinent question he could flash it forth and say: " Stand back! I am an American citizen!" After a week in London we went to the bank to draw some more money. The first man handed in his letter of credit and said: " If necessary, I have a pass——"

Before he could say any more the cashier reached out a little scoop shovel loaded with sovereigns and said: " Twenty pounds, sir."

We never could find a banker who wanted to look at our passports or who could be induced to take so much as a glance at them. I said to one banker: "We have our passports in case you require any identification." He said: "Rully, it isn't necessary, you know. I am quite sure that you are from Chicago."

We couldn't determine whether this was sheer

courtesy on his part or whether we were different.

After we were on the continent we hoped that some policeman would come to the hotel and investigate us, so that we could smile coolly and say: " Look at that," at the same time handing him the blue envelope. Then to note his dismay and to have him apologise and back out. But the police never learned that we were in town.

As for the art galleries and palaces, we had believed the handbook. We fancied that some day or other one of us would approach the entrance to a palace and that a gendarme would step out and say: " Pardon, monsieur, but the palace is closed to all visitors to-day."

" To most visitors, you mean."

" To all, monsieur."

" I think not, do you know who I am? "

" No, monsieur."

" Then don't say a word about anything being closed until you find out. I am an American. Here is my passport. Fling open the doors! "

At which the gendarme would prostrate himself and the American would pass in, while a large body of English, French and German tourists would stand outside and envy him.

66

Alas, it was a day-dream. Every palace that was closed seemed to be really closed, and when we did find the gendarme who was to be humiliated, we discovered that we couldn't speak his language, and, besides, we felt so humble in his presence that we wouldn't have ventured to talk to him under any circumstances.

We travelled in England, Ireland, Holland, Belgium, Germany, Switzerland, Italy, and France, crossing and recrossing frontiers, and we never encountered a man, woman or child who would consent to look at our passports.

On the other hand, the cable code is something that no tourist should be without. Whenever he is feeling blue or downcast he can open the code book and get a few hearty laughs. Suppose he wishes to send a message to his brother in Toledo. The code permits him to concentrate his message into the tabloid form and put a long newsy letter into two or three words. He opens the blue book and finds that he can send any of the following tidings to Toledo:

Adjunctio—Apartments required are engaged and will be ready for occupation on Wednesday.

Amalior—Bills of lading have not been endorsed.

Animatio—Twins, boy and girl, all well.

Collaria—Received invitation to dinner and theatre.

Illaqueo—Have a fly at the station to meet train arriving at eight o'clock.

Napina—Machinery out of order. Delay will be great.

Remissus—Can you obtain good security?

And so on, page after page. Theoretically, this vest pocket volume is a valuable helpmate, but when Mr. Peasley wanted to cable Iowa to have his Masonic dues paid and let Bill Levison take the river farm for another year and try to collect the money from Joe Spillers, the code book did not seem to have the proper equivalents.

We had with us on the boat an American who carried a very elaborate code book. All the way up from Plymouth to London he was working on a cablegram to his wife. When he turned it over to the operator, this is the joyous message that went singing through the water back to New York:

" LIZCAM, New York. Hobgoblin buckwheat explosion manifold cranberry suspicious.

" JAMES."

He showed us a copy and seemed to be very proud of it.

" That's what you save by having a code," he explained.

" What will Lizcam think when he receives that? "

" He? That's my wife's registered cable address. ' Liz ' for Lizzie and ' Cam ' for Campbell. Her maiden name was Lizzie Campbell."

" Well, what does that mean about a buckwheat hobgoblin having a suspicious explosion? "

" Oh, those words are selected arbitrarily to represent full sentences in the code. When my wife gets that cable she will look up those words one after the other and elaborate the message so that it will read like this:

He showed us the following:

" Mrs. Chauncey Cupple, Mount Joy Hotel, New York —— Dear Wife: Well, here we are at London, after a very pleasant voyage, all things considered. We had only two days of inclement weather and I was not seasick at any time. We saw a great many porpoises, but no whales. The third day out I won the pool on the run. Formed the acquaintance of several pleasant people. (Signed) James."

" It's just as good as a letter," said the man from Buffalo.

" Yes, and I save fifty-eight words," said Cupple. " I wouldn't travel without a code."

" Why don't you tack on another word and let her

know how many knots we made each day?" asked the Buffalo man, but his sarcasm was wasted.

A week later I met Mr. Cupple and he said that the cablegram had given his wife nervous prostration.

Mr. Cupple is not a careful penman and the cable operator had read the last word of the message as "auspicious" instead of "suspicious." A reference to the code showed that the mistake changed the sense of the message.

"*Suspicious*—Formed the acquaintance of several pleasant people.

"*Auspicious*—After a futile effort to work the pumps the captain gave orders to lower the boats. The passengers were in a panic, but the captain coolly restrained them and gave orders that the women and children should be sent away first."

The message, as altered in transmission, caused Mrs. Cupple some uneasiness, and, also, it puzzled her. It was gratifying to know that her husband had enjoyed the voyage and escaped seasickness, but she did not like to leave him on the deck of the ship with a lot of women and children stepping up to take the best places in the boat. Yet she could not believe that he had been lost, otherwise, how could he have filed a cablegram at London?

70

She wanted further particulars, but she could not find in the code any word meaning "Are you drowned?"

So she sent a forty-word inquiry to London, and when Mr. Cupple counted the cost of it he cabled back:

"All right. Ignore code."

CHAPTER VI

WHAT ONE MAN PICKED UP IN LONDON AND SENT BACK TO HIS BROTHER

A MAN is always justly proud of the information vhich has just come to hand. He enjoys a new piece of knowledge just as a child enjoys a new Christmas toy. It seems impossible for him to keep his hands off of it. He wants to carry it around and show it to his friends, just as a child wants to race through the neighbourhood and display his new toy.

Within a week the toy may be thrown aside, having become too familiar and commonplace, and by the same rule of human weakness the man will toss his proud bit of information into the archives of memory and never haul it out again except in response to a special demand.

These turgid thoughts are suggested by the behaviour of an American stopping at our hotel. He is here for the first time, and he has found undiluted joy in getting the British names of everything he saw. After forty-eight hours in London he was gifted with a new vocabulary, and he could not withstand the temptation to let his brother at home know all about it. The letter which he wrote was more British than any Englishman could have made it.

In order to add the sting of insult to his vainglorious display of British terms he inserted parenthetical explanations at different places in his letter. It was just as if he had said, " Of course, I'll have to tell you what these things mean, because you never have been out of America, and you could not be expected to have the broad and comprehensive knowledge of a traveller."

This is the letter which he read to us last evening:

" DEAR BROTHER: I send you this letter by the first post (mail) back to America to let you know that I arrived safely. In company with several pleasant chaps with whom I had struck up an acquaintance during our ride across the pond (ocean) I reached the landing stage (dock) at Southampton at 6 o'clock Saturday. It required but a short time for the examination of my box (trunk) and my two bags (valises), and then I booked (bought a ticket) for London. My luggage (baggage) was put into the van (baggage car) and registered (checked) for London. I paid the porter a bob (a shilling, equal to 24 cents in your money), and then showed my ticket to the guard (conductor), who showed me into a comfortable first-class carriage (one of the small compartments in the passenger coach), where I settled back to read a London paper, for which I had paid tuppence (4 cents in your money). Directly (immediately after) we started I looked out of the window, and was deeply interested in this first view of the shops (small retail establishments) and the frequent public houses (saloons). Also we passed through the railway yards, where I saw many drivers (engineers) and stokers (firemen) sitting in the locomotives, which did not seem to be as large as those to which you are accustomed in America.

"Our ride to London was uneventful. When we arrived at London I gave my hand luggage into the keeping of a porter and claimed the box which had been in the van. This was safely loaded on top of a four-wheeled hackney carriage (four-wheeled cab), and I was driven to my hotel, which happened to be in (on) the same street, and not far from the top (the end) of the thoroughfare. Arrived at the hotel, I paid the cabby (the driver) a half-crown (about 60 cents in your money), and went in to engage an apartment. I paid seven shillings (about $1.75) a day, this to include service (lights and attendance), which was put in at about 18 pence a day. The lift (elevator) on which I rode to my apartment was very slow. I found that I had a comfortable room, with a grate, in which I could have a fire of coals (coal). As I was somewhat seedy (untidy) from travel, I went to the hair-dresser's (the barber), and was shaved. As it was somewhat late I did not go to any theatre, but walked down the Strand and had a bite in a cook-shop (restaurant). The street was crowded. Every few steps you would meet a Tommy Atkins (soldier) with his ' doner ' (best girl). I stopped and inquired of a bobby (policeman) the distance to St. Paul's (the cathedral), and decided not to visit it until the next morning.

" Yesterday I put in a busy day visiting the abbey (Westminster) and riding around on the 'buses (omnibuses) and tram cars (street cars). In the afternoon I went up to Marble Arch (the entrance to Hyde Park), and saw many fashionables; also I looked at the Row (Rotten Row, a drive and equestrian path in Hyde Park). There were a great many women in smart gowns (stylish dresses), and nearly all the men wore frock coats (Prince Alberts), and top hats (silk hats). There are many striking residential mansions (apartment houses) facing the park, and the district is one of the most exclusive up west (in the west end of London). Sunday evening is very dull, and I looked around the smoking-room of the hotel. Nearly every man in the room had a ' B and S ' (brandy and soda) in front of him, although some of them preferred ' polly ' (apollinaris) to the soda. A few of them drank fizz (champagne); but, so far as I have observed, most of the Englishmen drink spirits (whiskey), although they very seldom take it neat (straight), as you do at home. I went to bed early and had a good sleep. This morning when I awoke I found that my boots (shoes), which I had placed outside the door the night before, had been neatly varnished (polished). The tub (bath) which I had bespoken (ordered) the night before was ready, and I had a jolly good splash."

We paused in our admiring study of the letter and remarked to the author that " jolly good splash " was very good for one who had been ashore only two days.

" Rahther," he said.

" I beg pardon? "

" Rahther, I say. But you understand, of course, that I'm giving him a bit of spoof."

" A bit of what? "

" Spoof—spoof. Is it possible that you have been here since Saturday without learning what ' spoof ' means? It means to chaff, to joke. In the States the slang equivalent would be ' to string ' someone."

"How did you learn it? "

" A cabby told me about it. I started to have some fun with him, and he told me to ' give over on the spoof.' But go ahead with the letter. I think there are several things there that you'll like."

So we resumed.

" For breakfast I had a bowl of porridge (oatmeal) and a couple of eggs, with a few crumpets (rolls). Nearly all day I have been looking in the shop windows marvelling at the cheap prices. Over here you can get a good lounge suit (sack suit) for about three guineas (a guinea is twenty-one shillings); and I saw a beautiful poncho (light ulster) for four sovereigns (a sovereign is a pound, or twenty shillings). A fancy waistcoat (vest) costs only twelve to twenty shillings ($3 to $5), and you can get a very good morning coat (cutaway) and waistcoat for three and ten (three pounds and ten shillings). I am going to order several suits before I take passage (sail) for home. Thus far I have bought nothing except a pot hat (a derby), for which I paid a half-guinea (ten shillings and sixpence). This noon I ate a snack (light luncheon) in the establishment of a licensed victualer (caterer), who is also a spirit merchant (liquor dealer). I saw a great many business men and clarks (clerks) eating their meat pies (a meat pie is a sort of a frigid dumpling with a shred of meat concealed somewhere within, the trick being to find the meat), and drinking bitter (ale) or else stout (porter). Some of them would eat only a few biscuit (crackers) for their lunch. Others would order as much as a cut of beef, or, as we say over here, a ' lunch from the joint.' This afternoon I have wandered about the busy thoroughfares. All the street vehicles travel rapidly in London, and you are chivied (hurried) at every corner."

" You have learned altogether too much," said Mr. Peasley. Where did you pick up that word ' chivy '? "

" I got that before I had been ashore a half hour. Didn't I hear one of those railroad men down at Southampton tell another one to ' chivy ' the crowd out of the custom house and get it on the train? I suppose that ' chivy ' means to rush or to hurry. Anyway, he won't know the difference, and it sounds about as English as anything I have heard over here."

The letter continued:

" One of the common sights in London is the coster's (costermonger's) little cart, drawn by a diminutive moke (donkey); but you do not see many of them west of the City (the original London confined within the boundaries of the ancient wall, but now comprising only a small part of the geographical area of the metropolis). I saw so many novel things that I would like to tell about them,

WHAT A MAN SENT HIS BROTHER

but I will reserve my further experiences for another letter."

"I don't want to write again until I have got a new stock of words," the author explained.

He read as follows in conclusion:

" This evening I am going to the theatre, having made a reservation (that is, having purchased) two orchestra stalls (parquet chairs) at the Lyceum. You may gather from this letter that I am having a ripping (very good) time, and in no hurry to terminate my stay in town (in London). I am your awfully devoted brother,

" ALEXANDER."

IN PARIS

CHAPTER VII

HOW AN AMERICAN ENJOYS LIFE FOR EIGHT MINUTES AT A TIME

THEY were all waiting for us—there at the corner, where the Avenue de l'Opera hooks on to the string of boulevards. They have been waiting for years without starving to death, so it is possible that once in a while some misguided American really employs one of them. They call themselves guides, but they are tramps—shabby genteel tramps, oiled and cheaply perfumed, full of shamefaced gayety, speaking wretched English. They come out of doorways at you, and in grovelling whispers beg of you to come with them and see all the wickedness of Paris. They attempt insulting familiarities, such as taking you by the arm or crowding close alongside and keeping up with you while they continue their blandishing arguments. Mr. Peasley expressed our violent emotions when he said: " When I'm tackled by one of those fellows I get hopping mad, because I know then that I must look easy."

We did not need any guide because we were looking

for a café, and without any particular effort on our part we found more than one thousand. On a crisp evening in February, with snow lying in the neglected corners, we should have hunted for a grate fire; but no, we were in Paris and we wanted to sit in front of a café. For a week Mr. Peasley had been saying, "Wait until we get to Paris and then we will go and sit in front of a café."

We saw many natives, all bundled up, sitting in the open street and slowly freezing to death, and so we joined one of the frigid little clusters and found some nice iron chairs waiting for us. It was a most heroic performance, but we took our coffee in the open air. A true Parisian can sit under a striped awning for hours at a time with nothing to entertain him except a few cigarettes, made of autumn leaves, and a large goblet filled with sweetened water. The newly arrived American wants to be truly Parisian, so he plants himself at a small table and settles back for an evening of calm enjoyment. In five minutes he has made a careful study of all the people at the neighbouring tables, he has watched the passing crowds until he is dizzy, and he is beginning to squirm and hanker for real excitement. He wants something to happen. It occurs to him that he is wasting time. He wonders if there isn't something doing a block or two to the east. So he moves on. By nine o'clock we had become sated with the café life of Paris and were scouting for a music hall.

When we were shown to our seats in the temple of art we found ourselves near three Americans, two sedate old men and a motherish woman in whom goodness and piety were plainly advertised. They were the kind of people who would not go to an entertainment in the church parlours at home unless assured by the pastor that the performance would be proper in all details. Here in Paris they sat in the front row of a music hall frequented by the gay characters of the boulevard and watched a pantomime which was calculated to peel the frescoes off the wall. They were not greatly amazed or shocked, but simply regarded the proceedings with sober interest. They were doing their plain duty as sight-seers.

Whenever I am in Paris I go to a show-shop in the evening and sit enthralled, listening to the musical singsong dialogue, of which I comprehended not one word. The pantomime gives an occasional flash-light on the story of the play and guess-work does the rest.

After making the rounds of the theatres, it is pleasant relaxation to watch the outdoor shows. I remember a travelling amusement enterprise that passed our hotel in the early morning of a fête day.

A big, square-shouldered fellow, with an overcoat almost concealing his suit of tights, was pulling a hand-cart containing a roll of carpet, some coils of rope, two chairs, several dumbells, and those worn blue-painted odds and ends that seem to litter the " show business " wherever it is encountered.

A smaller man, who did not wear tights, but whose attire, by its faded jauntiness, suggested his connection with the profession, walked behind the cart and pushed, although it seemed at times that he leaned more than he pushed.

Last of all came a stocky and erect young fellow, with a muscular frame dignifying an over-worn suit of clothes. He carried a valise and one did not need to see it open to know that it contained the powder, grease-paint, comb and brush, pocket mirror and bar of soap that accompany the entertainer on his travels and abide with him so long as hope remains.

Later in the day the aggregation was seen again, and this time at its best.

A crowd had formed a fringe around an open space in one of the boulevard " places " and was watching a performance. The big man who had pulled the cart seemed to be the workhorse of the company.

His smaller companion, who had held to the cart,

was now transformed into a clown, with baggy costume and painted face.

With much grunting and some grinding of the teeth the big man lifted dumb-bells into the air and held them there. His face was moist with perspiration and around the belt line of his tights there were damp spots.

When he had shown his prowess with dead weights he gathered up the stocky man, who was also in tights, and held him at arm's length above his head while his broad abdomen heaved like bellows.

The crowd was moved to applause, whereupon the clown, taking quick advantage of the demonstration, began passing the hat. The clown's duties were very simple. He made confidential remarks to the spectators, evoked some laughter by his comments on the various feats, and watched his opportunity to reach for the coppers. The big man worked incessantly, but the clown seemed to be the more popular with the lounging sight-seers. He had taken the safe attitude of a critic, and he must have known the secrets of business welfare. He allowed his associates to do the heavy work while he kept cool and gathered in the money.

One evening while passing a row of canvas booths on one of the open play-grounds we saw a young man with his hat off and his hair roughed up, taking deliberate aim with a rifle at a very small target twenty feet distant. The target was placed above a miniature prison about two feet high. Extending from the prison gate was a broad platform, on which was erected a guillotine perhaps eighteen inches high.

Evidently there was some hidden connection between the small target and the puny prison. The young Frenchman seemed unable to hit the target. First the bullet would strike just below and then just above or off at one side. He became discouraged once and started away, but this was too much like surrender, so he came back, paid for three more shots and vowed that he would not give up until he had succeeded.

On the second shot there was a sudden buzzing, and then the striking of a bell, which announced that he had hit the target. The prison doors flew open and out came three figures abreast, moving with slow and jerky deliberation.

The Frenchman who had invoked the spectacle dropped the gun and shouted with joy. At last he was to see it!

The three figures continued to move with mechanical gait toward the guillotine, and it could be seen that the bareheaded doll in the middle had its hands

88

tied behind it and that the printed lines of the face expressed mournful resignation. The two other men were fiercely bearded and appeared to be cruel and determined.

As they came to the guillotine the figure in the middle toppled forward without bending a joint and lay with its head in the groove of the block. This was time to turn away, sick at heart; but the Frenchman, who had spent as much as a franc to see this show, giggled with elation.

One of the bearded manikins raised his arm as if it were the handle of a pump. The tin blade fell, and the head, which was as large as a hickory nut, rolled into the basket.

Liberty, equality and fraternity! The reign of terror—three shots for ten centimes.

CHAPTER VIII

A CHAPTER OF FRENCH JUSTICE AS DEALT OUT IN THE DREYFUS CASE

A GOOD many people do not understand the method of French courts of law. Take the Dreyfus case, for instance. It has been dragging along for years, and the more evidence accumulated by Captain Dreyfus to prove his innocence, the greater seems to be his portion of woe. He has been vindicated over and over again and the vindications simply make him more unpopular with those who prefer to regard him as a mysterious and melo-dramatic villain.

People living at home have never understood why Captain Dreyfus was convicted in the first place. That is because they are not familiar with the work-ings of a French court and cling to the Anglo-Saxon rule, that every man must be regarded as innocent until he is proven guilty. The French say that trials may be greatly simplified if the presumption of guilt is attached to every defendant in a criminal case.

When the presumption of guilt is combined with a personal unpopularity, the prisoner usually finds it advisable to throw himself on the mercy of the court and accept a life sentence.

In order to elucidate the rules of procedure in a French court and show how and why Captain Dreyfus was convicted, let us suppose that French methods could be transferred to the United States and applied to an ordinary criminal case—say the theft of a dog. Here is what would happen.

The Court—" Prisoner, you are accused of stealing a dog. Are you guilty or not guilty? "

Prisoner—" Not guilty."

Court—" Well, someone stole a dog, and if you refuse to acknowledge your guilt, we may be compelled to cast suspicion on gentlemen who would be deeply pained to have themselves interrogated.

The Prisoner—" How can I acknowledge my guilt when I didn't steal the dog? "

Court—" That isn't the point. The point is that a great many prominent and influential people have said at different times that you stole the dog. Now, if you come before the tribunal and prove that you didn't steal the dog you are going to humiliate a great many well known and sensitive persons and make the whole situation very distressing to me. It

would simplify matters greatly if you would admit
that you stole the dog."

The Prisoner—" But how can I admit stealing the
dog when I am entirely innocent? "

The Court—" Did you ever see the dog said to have
been stolen? "

Prisoner—" Yes, sir." (Profound sensation.)

Court—" And yet you have the audacity to stand
there and say you didn't steal it? "

Prisoner—" A great many other people saw the
dog."

Court—" Perhaps so; but they would make
trouble if you or anyone else began insinuating
against them, so I don't propose to have their names
hauled in here. Of all the men who saw the dog and
had a chance to steal it, you are the only one whose
conviction would satisfy the general public."

Prisoner—" I can bring witnesses who saw another
man steal the dog. I can prove that he confessed to
stealing the dog and that he has fled to escape
punishment."

Court—"You ought not to bring any such testimony into this court, for if you do so you are going
to upset some theories held by very dear friends of
mine, and if I permit the introduction of such testimony, there is no telling what they will say about me.

If you didn't steal the dog isn't there something else you have done that is punishable in one way or another? "

Prisoner—" I can't think of anything just now."

Court—" Oh, pshaw! Aren't you guilty of something? Just think a moment. Nearly every man is guilty of something. If we can find you guilty of any old crime it will help some."

Prisoner—" I refuse to acknowledge any degree of guilt. I am innocent."

Court—" I don't see how you can be when so many estimable people think otherwise, but I suppose we shall have to give you a trial. Call the first witness."

First Witness—" Your Honor, I am a very high-minded and aristocratic person, and I have always disliked this defendant. (Sensation.) As soon as I had heard that someone had accused him of stealing a dog, I knew he must be guilty. I still hold to the opinion that he is guilty. I know that another man has confessed to stealing the dog, and has skipped out in order to avoid arrest, but these details have no weight with me. I am satisfied that if the defendant did not steal the dog mentioned in this affidavit, he must have stolen some other dog that we know nothing about. Ever since this wretched defendant was first accused of this crime I have been going around saying that he was guilty beyond the shadow of a doubt. Naturally I am not going to come here now and acknowledge his innocence. If he is acquitted, I'll be the subject of ridicule. That is why I urge the court to convict him. No matter what the testimony may show, you take my personal assurance that he is guilty. Remember one thing, that I have a large pull.

The Court—" Thank you very much for your testimony. Call the second witness."

Second Witness—" Your Honor, one day last spring I met a man whose friend told him that one day he saw the defendant pass the house from which the dog was stolen. From that moment I became convinced of the defendant's guilt. (Terrific sensation.) Another day a stranger walked into my office and told me that ' D ' was the first letter of the name of the man who stole the dog. Although there are 100,000 persons in town whose names begin with ' D,' I had no difficulty in coming to the conclusion that the particular ' D ' who stole the dog was the scoundrel now on trial. The reason that I came to this conclusion was that he used to wear a red necktie, and I dislike any man who wears a red necktie. Also I attach great importance to the fact that the letter ' D,' which is the first letter in his name, is also the first letter in 'Dog,' thus proving that he stole the dog. (Profound sensation.) In conclusion I would like to request the court to bring in a verdict of guilty.

The Court—"We will now have some expert testimony."

First Expert—"Your Honor, I never saw the prisoner before, and I had no personal acquaintance with the dog, but I am convinced that he stole the dog, and I will tell you why. You know, of course, that another man has confessed to stealing the dog. My theory, evolved after much thought, is that the man who confessed did not steal the dog at all, but that the dog was stolen by the defendant, who disguised himself so as to resemble the man who has confessed. (Great sensation.) There seems to be a universal admission that the man who stole the dog was a brunette. Some people claim that this fact points to the innocence of the defendant, who is a blonde; but my theory is that the defendant dyed his hair and whiskers so as to cause them to resemble the hair and whiskers of a certain innocent man, then he borrowed a suit of the innocent man's clothes and went and stole the dog, and the resemblance was so perfect that even the innocent man and the dog were both deceived. The innocent man thought that he,

95

and not the defendant, had stolen the dog, so he confessed and then ran away. But I am here to save him in spite of his confession. I maintain that if this defendant were to dye his hair and whiskers and put on a suit of clothes belonging to the man who has confessed to stealing the dog, then to anyone a short distance away he would bear a striking resemblance to the man who has confessed. Therefore the dog was not stolen by the man who has confessed, but by this infamous defendant cleverly disguised to resemble the man who has confessed."

The Court—" Then you think he is guilty? "

Expert Witness—" If there is anything in my theory, it is simply impossible for him to be innocent."

The Court—" Much obliged. Call the next witness."

Next Witness—" I would like to state to the court that the defendant is not very well liked down in our neighbourhood, where he formerly resided, and if the court will only convict him it will be a distinct personal favour to several of us."

The Court—" Do you think him guilty? "

Next Witness—" I haven't the slightest doubt of it. Neither has my wife. I have been convinced of his guilt ever since I heard him say one morning, ' I have something to do this afternoon.' It is evident to my mind that when he said, ' I have something to do this afternoon,' he meant, ' I am going to steal a dog this afternoon.' (Sensation.)

The Court—" Then you are quite sure that he did steal the dog? "

Next Witness—" Of course."

The Court—" Are there any other witnesses? "

Prisoner—" I have several witnesses here who saw the other man steal the dog. I can prove that at the time of the stealing I was ten miles away, attending a picnic. I can prove, also, that I didn't need a dog; that I never liked dogs; that I had no earthly motive for stealing a dog; and that from the time of my first accusation I have consistently and emphatically denied any knowledge of the crime."

The Court—" Well, I don't see that the dog has anything to do with the case. I'll sentence you to six months in the bridewell for being so blamed unpopular."

CHAPTER IX

THE STORY OF WHAT HAPPENED TO AN AMERICAN CONSUL

IN undertaking a trip to foreign parts I have had two objects in view:—

(a) To strengthen and more closely cement our friendly relations with foreign Powers—I to furnish the cement.

(b) To reform things in general over here.

I found that there was no opening for a real reformer in the U. S. A., inasmuch as the magazines were upsetting municipal rings, cornering the Beef Trust, and camping on the trail of every corporation that seemed to be making money. I said:—" If I wish to make a ten strike as a reformer I must seek new fields."

So I decided to flit to Europe and spend all the time I could spare from dodging *table d'hôte* dinners to bolstering up and regulating the consular service.

In writing to-day about the happy experiences of

an American consul I am following the advice of a friend who urged me to send some letters back home.

" Don't put in too much about your travels," he said. " People have read about European travel until they know Munich better than they do Montana. Whenever the opportunity presents itself write something entirely irrelevant—something that has nothing to do with anything in particular. The less you say about foreign countries the better you will please your readers, and if you can arrange to write a series of letters in which no reference is made to either Europe or Africa who knows but what you will score a hit? "

With no desire to boast of my accomplishments, I feel that up to date I have followed instructions rather closely. If any dates, statistics, or useful information have crept into these communications it is through oversight and not by intention.

In writing from Paris the natural impulse is to describe Napoleon's tomb and tell how the Champs Elysées runs right out to the Arc de Triomphe and then cuts through the Bois de Boulogne. Fearing that this subject matter had been touched upon by other visitors, I shall disregard Paris and go straight to my task of reforming the consular service.

To begin with, usually the American Consul is all right in his place, but his place is at home. Overpaid, possibly, but he does his best to earn his $800 per annum. If he kept all the money that he handled in the course of the year, he couldn't be a really successful grafter. He finds himself plumped down in a strange country. About the time that he begins to learn the language and has saved up enough money to buy evening clothes he is recalled and goes back home with a " dress suit " on his hands. Take the case of Mr. Eben Willoughby, of Michigan. It is a simple narrative, but it will give you a line on the shortcomings of our consular service, and it will carry its own moral.

" Old Man " Willoughby, as he was known at home, owned and edited a successful daily paper on the outskirts of the Michigan pine belt. He was a wheel horse in the party and for forty years had supported the caucus nominees. The aspiring politician who wished to go to Congress had to go and see Willoughby with his hat in his hand. He helped to make and unmake United States Senators and was consulted regarding appointments. But he never had asked anything for himself. His two boys went to college at Ann Arbor, and when the younger came home with his degree and began to take a hand in running the paper Mr. Willoughby found himself, for the first time in his life, relieved of wearing responsibilities. He was well fixed financially and still

Had to go and see Willoughby

in the prime of life—not due to retire permanently, but ready to take it easy. For years he had nursed a vague desire to travel beyond the limits of his native land. Mrs. Willoughby, who in the home circle was known as " Ma," was a devotee of the Chau-

101

tauqua Circle, and she, too, had an ambition born
of much reading to pack up and go somewhere. The
family doctor said that a visit to some milder climate,
far from the rigours of northern winter, would be
a positive benefit to her.

So Mr. and Mrs. Willoughby began to study the
atlas. One of the sons suggested to " Old Man "
Willoughby that he could take a trip to an attractive southern country at the minimum expense by se-
curing an appointment as consul. And, of course,
apart from the financial advantage, there would be
the glory of representing a great nation and hoisting the flag over a benighted foreign population.
The suggestion appealed very strongly to Mr. Willoughby. He wrote to the Congressman and the Sen-
ator, and wanted to know if there was a vacancy—
salary no object, but he would like to go into a mild
and equable climate where he could pick cocoanuts.

His friends at Washington simply overturned the
State Department in their eagerness to give him what
he wanted. They discovered that there was somewhere on the map a city called Gallivancia. It was
down by the southern seas—the abode of perpetual
summer and already enjoying a preliminary boom as
a resort. The acting consul had been a British subject. The pay was so small that no enterprising

American had wanted the job. " United States Consul at Gallivancia " reverberated pleasantly in the imagination of Mr. Willoughby. He told his friends at Washington to go after the place, and in less than no time his daily paper announced that he had " accepted " the appointment.

The politicians represented to the State Department that Mr. Willoughby was a sturdy patriot of unimpeachable character and great ability—all of which was true. They might have added that he would be just as much at home in Gallivancia as a polar bear would be on India's coral strand.

The news of his appointment gave one section of Michigan the trembles for several days, and the Willoughby family was bathed in a new importance. Mrs. Willoughby was given a formal farewell by the ladies of the congregation assembled in the church parlours. Mr. Willoughby was presented with a jewelled badge by the members of his lodge, and the band serenaded him the night before he went away.

He and " ma " stood on the back platform and gazed with misty eyes at the flutter of handkerchiefs on the station platform until the train swung around a curve and they found themselves headed straight for Gallivancia and glory. Both of them felt a little heart-achey and dubious, but it was too late to back out. At New York they boarded a ship and after several days of unalloyed misery they landed at Gallivancia.

Now, Gallivancia is the make-believe capital of a runt of an island having no commercial or other importance. No matter where an island may be dropped down, some nation must grab it and hold it for fear that some other nation will take charge of it and pay the expenses. That is why Gallivancia had a governor general and a colonel in command, and the Right Honourable Skipper of the gunboat and a judge and a cluster of foreign consuls. The men had a club at which whiskey and water could be obtained, unless the bottle happened to be empty. The women exchanged calls and gave formal dinners and drove about in rickety little victorias with terrified natives in livery perched upon the box. The lines of social precedence were closely drawn. At a dinner party the wife of the governor preceded the wife of the military commander who, in turn, queened it over the wife of the gunboat, who looked down upon the wife of the magistrate, and so on. The women smoked cigarettes and gambled at bridge, while every man who had won a medal at a shooting match pinned it on his coat when he went to a ball. It was a third-rate copy of court life, but these small dignitaries went through the motions and got a lot of fun out of it in one way and another. If we cannot afford a social position that is real ivory, the next best thing is to get one that is celluloid. It had all the intricate vices of a true nobility without the bona fide titles to back them up and give the glamour.

Into this nest of pretentious, ceremonious, strutting little mortals came " Old Man " Willoughby and " Ma " Willoughby of Michigan. Of the outward form and artificialities of a Europeanised aristocratic society they were most profoundly ignorant. Mr. Willoughby did not even own a " dress suit." When he got a clean shave and put on a string tie and backed into a " Prince Albert " coat he felt that he had made a very large concession to the mere fripperies of life. And " Ma " had her own ideas about low-necked gowns.

Can you see Mr. and Mrs. Willoughby in Gallivancia? Can you understand what must have been the attitude of these gold-braid pewees toward an old-fashioned apple pie couple from the tall timber?

Mind you, I am not poking fun at the Willoughbys. In the opinion of every real American a man of the Willoughby type is worth a ten-acre lot full of these two-by-four titles. The Willoughbys were

" D'yuh me! "

good people—the kind of people one likes to meet in Michigan. But when the ladies of the foreign colony came to call on " Ma " and said " Dyuh me! " and looked at her through their lorgnettes, she was like a staid old Plymouth Rock hen who suddenly finds herself among the birds of paradise. She told Mr. Willoughby that it was the queerest lot of " women folks " she had ever seen, and although she didn't like to talk about people until she knew her ground, some of them did not seem any more respectable than the law allowed. Poor Mrs. Willoughby! She did not know it was good form for a woman to smoke and drink, but bad form for her to be interested in her husband. She tried to apply a Michigan training to Gallivancia conditions, and the two didn't seem to jibe.

If Mrs. Willoughhby amused the women, Mr. Willoughby more than amused the men. He upset them and left them gasping.

The Acting Consul had used a small office adjoining his own place of business on the water front. Mr. Willoughby called on the former consul and found him to be a dignified Britisher of the gloomy and reticent sort, with a moustache shaped like a horseshoe. The dethroned official was courteous, but not cordial. He was saying good-by to some easy money, and the situation was not one calculated to promote good cheer. Mr. Willoughby's action in coming down and pulling the Consulate from underneath him seemed to him almost unfriendly. However, he formally turned over to Mr. Willoughby a table, four chairs, several account books, and a letter press, all being the property of the United States of America.

Mr. Willoughby had rented a house on the hill overlooking the town and decided to plant the Consulate in the front room of his residence. Inasmuch as the Consul had a business caller about once a month, there was no need of maintaining two establishments. Already he had taken into his employ and his warmest personal friendship a native named Franciotto. This name seemed formal and hard to remember, so Mr. Willoughby rechristened him " Jim." He liked this native in spite of his colour because he was the only man in Gallivancia who seemed to be pervaded by the simple spirit of democracy. Mr. Willoughby said that the others put on too many " damlugs "—whatever that may mean.

If U. S. Consul Willoughby's social standing in Gallivancia was at all subject to doubt that doubt vanished on the day when he and " Jim " came down to move the office effects to the house on the hill.

Mr. Willoughby did something that day which convulsed Gallivancia as it never had been convulsed before—not even when a neighbouring volcano blew off. For days afterward the official set, the men at the little club, and the women pouring tea at each other, talked of nothing else. Many would not believe when they first heard it, but there were witnesses —reliable witnesses—who saw the whole thing and were called upon time and time again to testify regarding the most extraordinary performance of the United States Consul. Other Consuls may come and go and the years spin their weary lengths and the obliterating drift of time may hide some of the lesser events in the history of Gallivancia, but until time shall be no more the residents of that city will tell the story of "Old Man" Willoughby, of Michigan.

What do you suppose he did? No effort of the imagination can carry you within hailing distance of the horrible truth, so let the suspense be ended. Mr. Willoughby, with his own hands, helped to move the furniture from the old Consulate up to his new residence. He put the table on top of his head and balanced it carefully and carried it through the open streets of Gallivancia! An official, a representative of a great Power, performing cheap manual labour!

Words are altogether inadequate to describe the

degree of obloquy which Mr. Willoughby earned for himself by this unheard-of exhibition. In Gallivancia it was not considered quite the thing to indulge in mental effort, and for anyone except a menial of the lowest social order to perform physical labour

What do you suppose he did?

was almost inconceivable. The new consul was set down as either a harmless imbecile or an altogether new specimen of barbarian. In either case he was not a fit associate for well-bred gentlemen, and Galli-

110

vancia proceeded to ignore him and " Ma." That is, they pretended to ignore them, but as a matter of fact, they watched them at a distance and heard daily reports of their familiarities with servants, their fondness for outlandish American cookery, and other eccentricities. It was all vastly diverting to the tiny aristocrats of Gallivancia, but it was pretty hard on Mr. and Mrs. Willoughby—homesick, hungry for spring chicken and garden truck, and yet ashamed to pick up and go home so soon after all those elaborate good-bys.

One morning Mr. Willoughby walked out on the veranda of his hillside cottage and looked across the harbour and saw something that smote him with an overpowering joy. A white cruiser, flying the Stars and Stripes, had steamed through the narrow entrance and was bearing down to an anchorage.

" Come here, mother! " he shouted. " Come here, if you want to see something that's good for sore eyes! "

Mrs. Willoughby came running, and nearly careened with happiness. There it was, an American war vessel, with real Yankees on board—boys from home; boys who had been brought up to believe that a man's character and his abilities give him a worth which cannot be altered by putting a mere handle to his name. Mr. and Mrs. Willoughby were eager to go down and call on the "folks from home." After the prolonged boycott which had been hanging over them they were pining for white society.

Mr. Willoughby put on his long black coat and Mrs. Willoughby got out her flowered bonnet and together they went down to the water front—walked instead of going as they should have gone, in one of the decrepit local hacks. Before they could charter a humble rowboat and go out to the ship the Governor General and the Lord High Commander of the Scow and the Imperial Collector of Customs and all the other residents of real importance had gone out in a launch and taken charge of the naval officers. Dinner parties and a ball at the "Palace" were arranged at once. The servant at the club hurried out and got another bottle of Scotch whiskey, and the town band began to mobilise at a café. Gallivancia had no use for a humble American of the Willoughby type, but it gave hysterical welcome to the splendid war vessel and the natty men in uniform. Over the first drink the Americans were told the remarkable story of the new Consul and were assured that he was a "queer sort." And the naval officers, being accustomed to hearing United States consuls maligned, took no further interest in their

112

government's representative; merely shook hands with him when he came aboard, told him to make himself at home, and then flocked away to the high lights and the gayety which had been provided for them by the court circles of Gallivancia.

Mr. and Mrs. Willoughby found themselves sidetracked, and they went back home not daring to talk about what had happened. But that was the day which caused them to decide to go back to Michigan. Mr. Willoughby wrote to the State Department and said that the climate did not agree with him. And when they sailed away " Jim " was the only person who came to the dock to bid them good-by.

As the " Ex-Consul to Gallivancia " Mr. Willoughby is more than ever an honoured figure in his own town.   Doubtless he has more gray matter, more Christian charity, and more horse sense than could be collectively assembled by all the petty officials at Gallivancia. And yet Gallivancia regarded him as a very poor excuse for a Consul. The naval officers saw in him a well-meaning " jay " who was bringing discredit on their native land because of his ignorance of social forms.

Therefore let us send out Consuls who can put up a " front." Have each Consul wear the uniform of a drum major. Make sure that he can dance all night, play bridge, and keep up with the naval crowd when it comes to drinking. Let him be haughty with the serving classes, but jovial with the military. Make sure that he is averse to all forms of labour. Such a Consul will shed glory upon our beloved country, and will never suffer the unhappy fate of " Old Man " Willoughby.

IN NAPLES

CHAPTER X

MR. PEASLEY AND HIS VIVID IMPRESSIONS OF FOREIGN PARTS

IN NAPLES—and Mr. Peasley is still with us.

We waited for him in London until he recovered his lost trunk, and he was so grateful that he decided to go along with us.

He said that he was foot-loose and without any definite plans and it always made him feel more at home to travel with people who were just as green and as much scared as he was.

A week ago we were in London—sloshing about in the damp and dismal mixture of mud and snow which lined the dark thoroughfares.

This morning we are basking in the crystal sunlight of Naples—the blue bay, with the crescent outline on one side, the white walls of the mounting city on the other, Vesuvius looming in the distance behind a hazy curtain, and tourists crowding the landscape in the immediate foreground.

Three big steamers are lying at anchor within the breakwater—one from Genoa, one from Marseilles,

Mr. Peasley is still with us

and one from New York—and all heavily laden with Americans, some sixty of whom will be our fellow-passengers to Alexandria. The hotels are overflowing with Yankee pilgrims, and every Neapolitan who has imitation coral and celluloid tortoise shell for sale is wearing an expectant smile.

The jack-rabbit horses attached to the ramshackle little victorias lean wearily in their shafts, for these are busy days. The harvest days are at hand. The Americans have come. An English woman who had seen the horde in the streets here remarked to a friend this morning, " It must be awfully lonesome in America just at present."

And she meant it, too.

It has been a fairly busy week for Mr. Peasley. Mr. Peasley is addicted to the habit of taking notes. Every night at the hotel he takes out a small leather-bound book presented to him by an insurance company in America in appreciation of the fact that he has paid the company all his ready money for the last fifteen years, and in this small volume he jots down brief memoranda.

Mr. Peasley has a terse style. Sometimes he uses abbreviations. His English is not of the most scholarly brand. As he is merely writing for himself, it makes no difference.

119

IN PASTURES NEW

The Peasley notebook, after twenty days in Europe, is full of meaty information, and contains many a flashlight on life in the Old World. By permission we are reproducing it herewith.

LONDON

" By Warrant.—Every man in London who sells anything, from a collar button to a chariot-and-four, does so 'by appointment' or 'by warrant.' Poor man opens shop—business bad. He is trying to sell shaving soap. One day royal personage floats in and buys a cake for 6d., whatever that means. Dealer puts out gold sign to the effect that he is supplying the royalty with lather. Public breaks down showcases getting at his merchandise. All true democrats theoretically ignore this second-hand worship of royalty, but, just the same, take notice that the shops with the rared-up unicorns in front and the testimonials from their Royal Majesties are the ones that catch the humble American tourist.

" Opera Hats.—Wandered into a hat store and discovered, to my amazement, that the proprietor was the inventor of the opera, or concertina, hat. Surprised—always supposed that at least a dozen men had worked on it. Establishment had documents to prove that the first folding hat had been manufactured on the very spot where I stood. Proprietor has not yet been knighted—probably an oversight.

"Rubber Pavement.—The large covered court of the Savoy Hotel is paved with blocks of soft rubber three feet square. Constant procession of cabs in and out of court, and rubber deadens sound. Good idea—should be used in all the streets of New York. New cab horse comes along—never has tackled rubber pavement—is clattering noisily over the asphalt—suddenly hits the soft rubber and begins to bounce up and down like a tennis ball. Strange look comes into horse's eye and he crouches like a rabbit, looks over his shoulder at the driver, and seems to be asking, 'What am I up against?' Mean trick to play on a green horse. Should be a warning sign displayed.

"Famine in Trousers.—One type of English chappy, too old for bread and jam and not quite old enough for music halls, wears extraordinary trousers —legs very narrow and reefed above tops of shoes (I mean boots)—causes them to look thin and bird-like.

"English Drama.—Saw new problem play last evening—new play, but same old bunch of trouble. Each principal character failed to marry the person

" What am I up against? "

of the opposite sex with whom he or she was really in love. Marriages did not interfere with love affairs, but helped to complicate the plot. Discovered why we can never have a great native drama in the States —we have no open fireplaces in which to destroy the incriminating papers. Impossible to destroy papers at a steam radiator.

"L. C. C.—In musical comedies, pantomimes, and at music halls, many sarcastic references to L. C. C., meaning London County Council. Council is ploughing open new streets, tearing down old buildings, putting up new buildings, and spending money like a sailor on a holiday. Their extravagance has given great offence to the low comedians and other heavy rate payers, while the very poor people, who are getting parks, sunshine and shower baths free of charge, bless the L. C. C. The dress coat crowd in the theatres seem to have it in for the L. C. C., but they are very strong for Mr. Chamberlain, notwithstanding his recent defeat. Mr. Chamberlain seems to be a great deal like Mr. Bryan—that is, nearly everyone admires him, but not enough people vote for him. In spite of protest from property holders, L. C. C. is going bravely ahead with gigantic task of modernising and beautifying London. Asked an Englishman why there was so much criticism of L. C. C. He said if you touch a Britisher in the region of his pocketbook he lets out a holler that can be heard in Labrador. Didn't use those words, but that's what he meant.

" Snowstorm.—Last night a few snowflakes drifted into Piccadilly Circus; hardly enough to cover the ground this morning, but everyone is talking about the ' snowstorm.' London is away ahead of us on fogs, but their snowstorms are very amateurish.

" Coals.—Buying my coal by the quart—forty cents a quart. If I fed the fire the way I do at home would spend $100 a day. The official who brings fuel to my room in a small tin measure insists upon calling it ' coals,' but I didn't think there was enough of it to justify use of plural.

PARIS

" Coming Across.—The turbine boat from Dover to Calais ran like a scared deer and rolled like an intoxicated duck. Held to rail all the way across, looking fixedly at oscillating horizon and wondering why I had left home—bleak, snowy landscape all the way from Calais to Paris. After dinner went to music hall and learned that Paris could be fairly warm, even in the dead of winter.

"Keeping Tab on the Cab.—The 'taximetre' cab is a great institution—small clockwork arrangement alongside of seat, so that passenger may sit and watch the indicator and know how his bill is running up. The indicator is set at seventy-five centimes at the start. In other words, you owe fifteen cents before you get away. Then it clicks up ten centimes at a time, and when you reach your destination there is no chance for an argument regarding the total. What they need now in Paris is a mechanism to prevent the driver from taking you by a roundabout.way.

"Just for Fun.—Strange epidemic of killing in Paris. Two or three murders every night, not for revenge or in furtherance of robbery, but merely to gratify a morbid desire to take life. Among certain reckless classes of toughs, or 'Hooligans,' it is said to be quite the fashion for ambitious characters to go out at night and kill a few belated pedestrians merely in a spirit of bravado and to build up a reputation among their associates. Seems unfair to the pedestrians. At one of the theatres where a ' *revue* ' or hodge-podge ' take-off ' on topics of current interest, was being presented, the new type of playful murderer was represented as waiting at a corner and shooting up, one after another, some twenty-five citizens who chanced to stray along. This performance was almost as good as the Buffalo Bill show and gave much delight to the audience.

"Costly Slumber.—From Paris to Marseilles is about as far as from Chicago to Pittsburg. Sleeping car fare is about $10; total fare by night train, about $30. Two cents a pound for all baggage in excess of a measly fifty-six pounds. No wonder people travel by day in the refrigerator cars and try to keep warm by crawling under hundreds of pounds of 'hand luggage.' Anything with a handle to it is 'hand luggage.' Some of the cowhide bags must have used up two or three cows.

"Tea Habit. The tea habit has struck Paris. At Grand Hotel and many cafés general round-up about five in the afternoon, everyone gulping tea and eating cakes. Not as demoralising as the absinthe habit, but more insidious.

"American Music.—After a 'coon' song has earned a pension in the United States it comes over to Paris and is grabbed up as a startling novelty. All the ' revues ' studded with songs popular at home about two years ago—Frenchmen believe that all Americans devote themselves, day in and day out, to accumulating vast wealth and singing coon songs.

"Oysters.—Went to famous fish and oyster res-

taurant for dinner. The Gallic oyster wears a deep
blush of shame and tastes like the day after taking
calomel. Thought horseradish might improve, mod-
ify or altogether kill the taste, so I tried to order
some. Knew that ' horse ' was ' cheveau ' and ' red '
was ' rouge,' but could not think of the French for
' ish,' so I had to do without. Somewhat discouraged
about my French. Almost as bad as former American Consul, who, after eight years in Paris, had to
send for an interpreter to find out what ' oui '
meant. Have got ' merci ' down pat, but still pronounce it ' mercy.'

" More Snow.—The further south we go the colder
the weather and the deeper the snow. Getting my
furs ready for Cairo. Ten hours on the train from
Paris to Marseilles, wrapped in a blanket and count-
ing the warts on a foreign commercial traveller who
sat opposite. No two counts agreed. Had looked forward during a long month to this ride through
sunny France. Had dreamed of green landscapes
that lay smiling in the genial warmth, the stately
poplars leading away to purple hills, and the happy
labourers looking up from their toil in the fields to
smile at us and bid us welcome as we flashed by. Not
a bit like it. More on the order of North Dakota.

Everybody says it is the coldest snap that Southern France has known in many years. They saved up all their cold weather so as to hand it to me when I came along.

" Bouillabaisse (spelling not guaranteed).—There is only one thing to do in Marseilles, and that is to drive out to an excellent restaurant built on a rock overlooking the bay and partake of bouillabaisse. Dish famed in song and story. Mentioned often in ' Trilby.' Possibly that is what ailed Svengali. The bouillabaisse and the ' Marseillaise ' were both invented in Marseilles. The mayonnaise comes from elsewhere. The bouillabaisse is a combination of soup, ragout, chowder, and New England boiled dinner. There are many ingredients. It is said they put in whatever they have the most of—sea bass, lobsters, crayfish, vegetables, sauces—everything except the license. Liked the taste very much—first when I ate it, and then all during the afternoon and evening.

" Chateau d'If.—Coming out of the harbour we ran very close to the Chateau d'If, a stern fortress prison topping a huge rock rising sharply from the bay. Count of Monte Cristo was imprisoned here. Man on board said that the character of Edmund Dantes was wholly fictitious, manufactured by Dumas. Must be a mistake, as I saw the small rock on

128

which James O'Neill used to stand at the end of the first act and exclaim, 'The world is mine!' It is exactly as represented on the stage, except for the calcium light.

NAPLES

"The Ship's Barber.—Coming across from Marseilles in the *dampfer* (Germ. for boat) the weather moderated so that I needed only one overcoat. Got acquainted with barber. Often have some trouble in making up with a captain, but can usually hit it off with the barber. A good barber is a bureau of information, headquarters for scandal, and knows what the run is going to be. The barber on our *dampfer* no good. Shy on conversation, but great on arithmetic. Charged me two francs for a shave, and when I suggested that he was rather high he said he was compelled to ask one franc and thirty centimes for the extract of vanilla he had put on my hair. Told him I did not want any extract of vanilla, but he said there was no way of getting it back into the bottle. Besides, he had the money, so we compromised by permitting him to keep it. Said he longed to go to America. I told him there would probably be an opening in America for anyone so energetic and muscular, and I promised to give him a letter to Armour & Co., of Chicago.

Promised him a letter to Armour & Co., Chicago

130

" Free Fireworks.—A full hundred miles out at sea we could make out an irregular oval of fire suspended in the sky—the two streams of lava now trickling down Vesuvius. Finest landmark and sailing target a sailor could ask for. When we were forty miles away we wanted the captain to slow up for fear he would run into the mountain and injure it. Next morning in harbour we discovered that we were still ten miles away from it.

" The New Naples.—In ten years Naples has done a lot of sprucing up. Streets are cleaner, new and pretentious buildings have multiplied, smells have been eliminated. Guides, beggars and cabmen not so pestiferous as of yore, but still bad enough to deserve electrocution, provided some more lingering form of death could not be substituted. Cabmen seemed downcast. Municipality recently forbade any extra charge for cab service on a *fiesta*, or holiday. In Italy 300 days out of every 365 can be rung in under the head of *fiestas*. Every American who landed in Naples found himself right in the midst of a *fiesta* and had to pay two fares, or as much as thirty cents in gold, to ride around in one of the open hacks. Thirty cents would seem a reasonable charge, but not after you have seen the hack. The smaller the horse in Naples the heavier the harness.

131

Evidently a desire to have about the same total weight in each case.

"Emigrants.—Alongside of our ship lay a German steamer about to sail for America. The tender made trips to and from the dock, and every time she came out she was filled to the last inch with Italian emigrants. We saw hundreds of them disappear into the ship, so many it seemed they must have been packed in below by hydraulic pressure, otherwise there wouldn't have been room for them. All headed for the land of the free to build railroads. Englishman wanted to know why there was such heavy emigrant traffic at this particular season. Told him they were hurrying over to vote at the April election in Chicago. He believed it. Come to think of it, I believe it myself."

This is Mr. Peasley's notebook up to the present moment, just as we are departing for Alexandria. He admits that he may have overlooked a few minor points of interest, but he more than made up by neglecting to mention Napoleon's tomb or the Moulin Rouge.

Since arriving in Naples this morning Mr. Peasley has arranged with the tourist agency to change his ticket, and he will accompany us to Egypt.

IN CAIRO

CHAPTER XI

CAIRO AS THE ANNUAL STAMPING GROUND FOR AMERICANS AND WHY THEY MAKE THE TRIP

"IT'S a small world."

This is one of the overworked phrases of the globe-trotter. It is used most frequently by those who follow the beaten paths. In other words, we find it difficult to get away from our acquaintances. Not that we wish to get away from them; on the contrary, when we are stumbling along some unfamiliar thoroughfare six thousand miles from home and bump into a man with whom we have a nodding acquaintance in Chicago, we fall upon his neck and call him brother. It must be very annoying to criminals and celebrities who are trying to hide their identities, but to the ordinary traveller it is always a glad surprise to find a friend coming right out of the ground in a corner of the world supposed to be given over to strangers.

There are certain spots on the earth which may be classed as definite headquarters for wanderers. It is said that in the summer season any person of any nationality who seats himself in front of the Café de la Paix in Paris may confidently gamble on hailing an acquaintance in less than fifteen minutes. Trafalgar Square, in London, is called by the Britishers the actual kernel of civilisation. The long corridor

Very annoying to criminals and celebrities

of the Waldorf is the temporary abode of folks from almost everywhere. The big " front porch " here at Shepheard's Hotel, in Cairo, will surely have two or three friends waiting for you when you arrive. The

Grand Hotel, in Yokohama, has been for many years a sort of clearing-house for travellers—circumnavigators moving aside to let the other crowd pass. Then there is (*was*, alas!) the Palace, in San Francisco, and the Auditorium, in Chicago—definite rallying points for mortals who move about.

It is when we meet our long-lost friend in the remote by-way that we are induced to throw up our hands and exclaim, " The world is small."

For instance, before the German steamer left Naples for Alexandria a launch load of new passengers came aboard. As we were heading out of the bay and almost under the shadow of Capri I glanced at the man in the adjoining steamer chair and recognised the banker from Tien-tsin. He was just as much surprised as I was.

About a year ago we parted at San Francisco after a long and pleasant voyage from Shanghai— he to continue a leisurely trip around the world, I to carry my priceless treasures of Oriental art and shattered letter of credit back to Indiana. When we parted there was the usual stereotyped remark about meeting again, but neither of us believed that there was one chance in a million of our paths crossing, it being a far cry from Tien-Tsin to Terre Haute. I don't know what a " far cry " is, but I have come across it in some of our most opaque dissertations, and accordingly I welcomed the opportunity to use it.

The man from Tien-Tsin had loitered in Europe and was now heading straight for China. I had made up my mind in a hurry to go to Egypt to help 10,000 other students investigate the tombs, and here we were, side by side, in the Mediterranean.

A few minutes after colliding with him I had the pleasure of meeting a young woman who said that she was the sister of Henry Billkamp, of Chicago. She asked me if I remembered the circumstances under which I met Henry, and I told her that I couldn't very well forget them.

A few years ago in Chicago I resided in a large establishment which had as an auxiliary feature a fine Turkish bath. Many of our best people would come to the bath every afternoon, first steaming themselves in the vapour room, then scrubbing themselves, then a shower, and after that a plunge—by which time most of the coal dust could be removed. Henry Billkamp came to the bath one afternoon and brought with him a suit case containing his evening clothes and accessories. Henry was to be married the next day, and that evening he and the bride elect were to be guests at a large dinner party on the south side. Henry looked at his watch and found that he could loll around the bath for an hour before jumping into his evening clothes. So he put his suit case over in one corner of a dressing-room, and in a few minutes had joined the informal circle which was commonly known as the " Perspiration Club."

It may be said in passing that Henry was a very estimable young man of first-class abilities and that he was built on the general outlines of a flagpole. He pierced the atmosphere for a considerable distance, in an up and down direction, but he never blocked the view of any person who chanced to be standing behind him.

While Henry Billkamp was in the steam chamber engaged in the superfluous task of further reducing himself, Bob Grimley came into the bath department carrying a suit case. The suit case habit is very strongly intrenched in busy towns. To go all the way out home and then come back would use up two hours.

Bob Grimley was a short man, weighing about two hundred and fifty pounds, and shaped like an olive. He wanted his vapour in a hurry, because he had to grab a train and go away out to Oak Park and then dress in a hurry and have a bite of dinner and play poker. So he made a running splash and jump through the bath department, came out, hopped into his garments, picked up Henry Billkamp's suit case, and rushed away to Oak Park.

It was half past six when Henry Billkamp arose from the plunge and hurried to the dressing-room. The dinner was to be at seven. He opened the suit case and began to take out balloon-shaped garments, and then he shrieked for an attendant. Where was his suit case? No one seemed to know. Oh, yes; Mr. Grimley had come out of that room with a suit case and had gone—no one knew whither. Henry stood there with a huge article of raiment clutched in each hand and slowly froze with horror as a full understanding of the situation grew upon him. In less than a half-hour he must join them—bride, relatives, friends. The lights were already up, the flowers on the table, the wine cooling, the carriages beginning to arrive. It was to be the night of his life. Could he appear at this glittering function as a chief attraction in an eight dollar sack suit and make some lame explanation about losing his other things in a Turkish bath? He had an old suit at home, but he was miles from home. The carriage man sent in word that Mr. Grimley and suit case had gone to a railway station. That settled it. Henry decided to jump into the plunge and end it all.

140

While he was lamenting, a friend came in from another dressing-room to find out what was the matter. Henry, scantily attired, leaned against the wall and in a voice choked with sobs and cuss words outlined his frightful predicament. The friend, listening, suddenly emitted a glad shout.

"I have it!" he exclaimed. "There's only one man in all the world with a figure anything like yours, and he happens to be right here in the building. Come! Get into a dressing gown. We have twenty minutes! We can make it. Come!"

A few seconds later two agitated persons, one attired and the other semi, burst into my room. It was a long story, but could they borrow an assortment of evening clothes? Could they? I was delighted to know that someone in the world wanted to wear that suit.

No fireman going to a fire ever dressed himself with such rapidity as we dressed the hysterical Henry. Everything fitted him perfectly. Shirt, collar, trousers, waistcoat, swallowtail, opera hat, tie, gloves, studs, buttons—everything just his size. Nothing in the outfit had ever fitted me, but when we got through with Henry he was beyond criticism. He actually wept with joy as we ran him out to the carriage and boosted him in and started him southward, with eleven minutes to spare. He arrived on the dot. For weeks afterward he would sit down every day and write me a letter of thanks and declare that he would never forget me and the service I had done him. Of course, it would have been impossible for me to forget anyone who had looked well in my evening clothes, and it was a positive pleasure to meet Henry's sister. She said she had long desired to have a look at me. She had not believed it possible that there was another living mortal whose clothes would fit Henry, but now she saw that she had been mistaken.

It is flattering to learn that people we have never met have been interested in us for a long time. Continuing the same line of thought, it is often disappointing to learn that the people most deeply interested in us are those who have never met us. For fear of getting mixed up, let us return to the boat.

Our principal cargo was honeymoon. We had six newly married couples, who were advertising to all the world the fact of their sudden happiness, and three other couples were under suspicion. The men lounged in the smoking-room, as if to give the impression that they were hardened in matrimony, but they peeked out through the portholes too often and made many trips to the deck.

One German couple was the most newly married team that any of us had ever seen. I don't think they knew they were in a boat. They may have suspected, but it really didn't make any difference. They were in a trance, riding on a cloud of incense, saturated

Three other couples under suspicion

with bliss. He was middle aged, with red flaring whiskers, and a nose showing an angular break in the middle. She was short and plump, with a shiny, oil-finish countenance. Neither had been constructed ac-

143

cording to the plans and specifications of Love's
Young Dream, and yet the devouring adoration
which played back and forth between Romeo and
Juliet was almost icy compared with this special
brand of Teutonic love. They were seldom more than
three inches apart, he gazing into her eyes with a
yearning that was unutterable (even in German) and
she gazing right back at him in blushing rapture and
seeming to say to herself:—" Just think! He belongs
to me, whiskers and all!" It was almost enough to
induce one to get married.

They were drifting so far above the earth that
they forgot to be seasick. The other honeymooners
took to their cabins.

Is there anything so perverse, so whimsical, so
tantalising, and so full of surprises as our old friend
the weather? When the warm sunshine trickled down
our backs in Naples we rejoiced and said, " At last
we have found summer." We looked forward to three
balmy days on the blue Mediterranean, and even began to remember where we had packed the summer
clothes at the bottom of the trunk. During the first
night out we passed between Scylla and Charybdis.
They sound like a team of acrobats, but really they
are the promontories guarding the narrow Strait of
Messina. It was pitch dark when we passed, and we

had turned in, but we read about them in Baedeker next morning and were much gratified to know that

" *—Whiskers and all* "

we had been so near them. Not that we can describe them, but hereafter we can refer to them.

After we rounded the south coast of Italy and

pointed for Alexandria, we ran into a mess of weather that had lost its bearings and wandered down from the north Atlantic. The wind blew a gale. We sat huddled in our heaviest wraps. The good ship pitched and pitched, and then pitched some more. And this was the Mediterranean! We had promised ourselves to lie basking in the gentle warmth and count the lateen sails as they went drifting by. We had expected to see the whole surface of the Mediterranean almost as busy as State and Madison, or Broadway and Forty-second—craft of all descriptions criss-crossing the blue ripples, a continuous aquatic bioscope. As a matter of fact, we rode for three days across waters as lonesome and empty as those of the north Pacific, where the course is so clear that the captain, after putting to sea, can tie the wheel and go below and play dominoes.

Our chilly voyage from Naples to Alexandria has suggested a few reflections on travel in general. Why the Anglo-Saxon passion for gadding about? Cairo to-day is absolutely congested with Americans. The continent of Europe is two days away by speedy boat; Paris is two days more, and London less than a week by ordinary modes of travel. America lies three thousand miles beyond the most remote European city and across stormy waters, and yet America

146

seems to claim a plurality of all the transients. If an Egyptian began to pack up his things to take a four thousand mile jump to look at the stock yards of Chicago or the Mammoth Cave of Kentucky, his friends would have him consigned to some Mohammedan institution for the treatment of those mentally deranged. But the Americans are here in flocks, droves, coveys—decrepit old people; blooming debutantes, boys just out of college, tired-out business men, women who have been studying Egypt at their clubs, and, of course, the 8000 (more or less) newly married couples. And most of them are working like farm hands to generate some real enthusiasm for tombs and hieroglyphics. Hard pulling, but they will make it if their legs hold out.

What is the charm—the siren call of Egypt—that has lured these thousands so far away from home and friends? It is not climate, for we have a better climate of our own. If the traveller seeks merely warmth and sunshine, he can find them in Southern California, the West Indies, or at Palm Beach. It is not a genuine and deep-seated interest in ancient records, inasmuch as ninety per cent. of the fresh arrivals from America do not know the difference between a cartouche and a scarab. I know, because I looked it up yesterday. It is not a snobbish desire to

rub up against the patchouli and rice powder of
European hothouse aristocracy, because nearly all
of the Americans flock by themselves and make dis-
paraging remarks about other nationalities, and vice
versa.

No doubt the one great reward of the persistent
traveller is to find new varieties of his fellow man.
Cairo is the *pousse café* of humanity—probably the
most cosmopolitan city in the world. The guide books
talk about rock tombs and mosques, but the travellers
find their real enjoyment in the bazaars and along the
crowded streets and on the sheer banks of the Nile,
which stand out as an animated panorama for hundreds of miles. The first hour in Cairo is compensation for many an hour of tedious travel. Once more
in the sunshine, the soft but gamey flavour of Orien-
talism soothing the nostrils, a lively chatter of unfamiliar languages; an interweaving throng of turbans,
gowns, fezes, swarthy faces; the pattering hoof-
beats of spangled donkeys and the stealthy sweep of
dignified camels—so much to see that one needs four
pairs of eyes to catch all parts of the picture and at
least a half-dozen fountain pens to keep score of the
attractions.

The first hour in a new land! It is that which
repays the patient traveller. It gives him the gasping

surprises and the twinges of delight which are not to be found in southern California or at Palm Beach. And it is the very first hour which is memorable and crowded with large emotions. Because, after about two hours, the American has adapted himself to his new environment, and is beginning to be blasé. Along about the second day, when the guide attempts to dazzle him by showing another variety of bazaar he murmurs " Chestnut " and suggests going back to the hotel.

It may afford consolation to the large number of people who remain at home to know that only about five per cent. of foreign travel is really worth while. Mr. Emerson's beautiful law of compensation holds true in regard to travel just as it applies to all other things that are coveted by mortals. You must pay for what you get, not in money alone, but in hardships, annoyances, and long periods of dumb, patient waiting.

The better half of one of the honeymoon combinations that came with us from Naples told a plaintive story. She had been travelling for three weeks in weather that had been a *crescendo* of the disagreeable. All the way across the Atlantic she had been desperately ill in her cabin. In London they found fogs. In Paris it rained. And now they were fighting their

149

way through a storm in the Mediterranean. Notwithstanding all this, she was trying to be cheerful, for she believed that she would like Egypt.

The blessedness of travel is that when the sun comes from behind the cloud and a new city begins to arise from the sea, we forget all the gloomy days on board ship, all the crampy rides in the stuffy railway compartments, all the overcharges and vexations and harassments and get ready to tear ashore and explore a new wonderland.

Who can forget the first hour of the first railway ride through rural England? The storybook pictures that you have seen all your life come true at last.

Or the first hour in London? That tall thing looming right in front of you is really the Nelson monument and not a papier maché deception put up for the entertainment of tourists.

In the first hour of 'rickshaw riding in Japan I saw so much that was funny and fantastic and nerve kinking that at the end of the ride I wanted to pay the coolie for a year instead of an hour.

And how about the first hour up the Grand Canal in Venice? Or the first hour in the tangled bedlam of Canton? Or the first hour in front of Shepheard's Hotel, here in Cairo, when it really seems that a wonderful pageant has been ordered for your special joy? With bulging eyes and reeling senses you view the changing kaleidoscope and ask, in the language of Mr. Peasley, " Is this on the level? "

Yes, travel is hard work, and your true traveller is a mighty grumbler, but he goes on buoyed always by the hope of another " first hour."

CHAPTER XII

ROUND ABOUT CAIRO, WITH AND WITHOUT THE ASSISTANCE OF THE DRAGOMAN OR SIMON LEGREE OF THE ORIENT

MR. PEASLEY is a secretive student of the guide book.

He reads up beforehand and on the quiet. Then when we come face to face with some " sight " and are wondering about this or that, Mr. Peasley opens the floodgate of his newly-acquired knowledge and deluges the whole party. He is seldom correct, and never accurate, but he knows that he is dealing with an ignorance more profound than his own, and that gives him confidence.

For instance, the first afternoon in Cairo we chartered an open conveyance and rode out to the citadel and the mosque of Mohammed Ali, both of which are perched on a high limestone cliff overlooking the city. The mosque is modern and very gorgeous with alabaster columns, a profusion of gay rugs, stained windows, and crystal chandeliers. We were rhapsodising over the interior and were saying it was almost as swell and elegant as the new Claypool Hotel in Indianapolis, when we happened to overhear one of our countrywomen reading aloud from a very entertaining book on Egypt written thirty years ago by Amelia B. Edwards. Miss Edwards allowed that the mosque of Mohammed Ali was a tawdry and hideous specimen of the most decadent period of the mixed-up architectures imported from Araby and Turkey. When we heard that we made a quick switch and began to find fault with the decorations and told the guide we had enough.

On the way out to the parapet to enjoy the really wonderful view of the city and the Nile Valley, with the pyramids lifting themselves dimly from the old gold haze of the desert, Mr. Peasley wished to repay the lady who had read to us, so he paused, and, making a very indefinite and non-committal gesture, said, "Near this very spot Mohammed Ali killed more than one hundred and fifty mamelukes in one day."

Our fair countrywoman looked at Mr. Peasley with a puzzled frown on her brow and then timidly asked, "What is a mameluke?"

We thought she had him, but not so. He wasn't even feazed. He replied promptly, "A mameluke is something like a mongoose, only larger."

That is Mr. Peasley's way. If he doesn't know, at

" What is a mameluke? "

154

least he will make a stab at it. One evening at dinner we had anchovies as a curtain raiser, and a man sitting next to Mr. Peasley poked at the briny minnows with his fork and asked, " What are these? "

" Those are anchorites," replied Mr. Peasley, without the slightest hesitation.

As a rule he gets one syllable right, which is pretty good for him. At present he is much interested in the huge dams of masonry and iron gates that have been thrown across the Nile at Assiut and Assouan. Over here they are called " barrages." Mr. Peasley insists upon calling them " garages." We tried to explain to him that a garage was a place where automobiles were cared for, but he said that automobile and " dam " belonged in the same category and often meant practically the same thing, so he continues to speak of the " garage."

By the way, when a pious Englishman over here, say a bishop on a vacation, wishes to relieve his feelings without the actual use of profanity he exclaims " Assouan! " If he falls off his donkey, " Assouan! " If his tea is served to him at less than 212 degrees Fahrenheit, " Assouan! "

" Assouan " means the superlative of all dams, the biggest dam in the world. It takes the place of a whole row of these:— ——— ——— —— ———.

Mr. Peasley uses the word, when he can think of it.
If his memory fails him, he falls back on the American equivalent.

Inasmuch as I reside in Indiana, where it is a
social offence to crave a cigarette, a misdemeanor to

Assouan!

keep one in the house, and a high crime to smoke one,
Cairo during the first day gave me many a shock.
Cairo is unquestionably the cigarette headquarters
of the universe. If the modern Egyptians followed

156

the ancient method of loading the tomb with supplies for the lately departed they would put in each sarcophagus about ten thousand cigarettes and a few gallons of Turkish coffee. The food wouldn't matter.

In Cairo, men, women, and children smoke. Only the camels and donkeys abstain.

Cigarettes are sold nearly everywhere—not only by tobacconists, but also by milliners, undertakers, real estate agents, etc. Those who do not sell them give them away. A cigarette across the counter is the usual preliminary to driving a bargain.

It surprised us to learn that although the Egyptians have been addicted to this enfeebling vice ever since they first had a chance to cultivate it, they have managed to survive and flourish as a distinct breed of humanity for some seven thousand years, as nearly as I can figure it off hand. By eliminating the cigarette from Indiana the Hoosiers should beat this record. No doubt they will retain their primitive vigour for a longer period, say nine thousand years. If so, the anti-cigarette law will be vindicated.

We certainly had a feeling of guilty pleasure when we sat in front of Shepheard's Hotel and smoked the wicked little things, and knew that the policeman standing a few feet away did not dare to raise his hand against us.

A very clever young American owns a shop near the hotel. He is a student of Egyptology and a dealer in genuine antiquities, including mummies. While I was nosing through his collection of scarabs, idols, coins, and other time-worn trinkets, he suggested that I purchase a mummy.

" Can I get one? " I asked, in surprise.

" I can get you a gross, if you want them," he replied.

" What would a man do with a gross of mummies? "

" You can give them away. They are very ornamental. Formerly my only customers were colleges and museums. Now I am selling to people who put them in private residences. Nothing sets off an Oriental apartment to better effect, or gives it more colour and atmosphere, as you might say, than a decorated mummy case."

I told him I would not object to the " colour," but would draw the line at " atmosphere." He assured me that after a few thousand years the mortuary remains become as dry as a London newspaper and as odourless as a Congressional investigation.

I followed him into a large back room and saw two beautifully preserved specimens in their rigid overcoats being packed away for shipment to America, while others leaned against the wall in careless attitudes.

What a grisly reflection! Here was a local potentate, let us say Ipekak II. of Hewgag—ruler of a province, boss of his party, proud owner of broad fields and grazing herds. When he died, 1400 B. C., and was escorted to his rock tomb by all the local secret societies, the military company, and a band of music, his friends lowered his embalmed remains into a deep pit and then put in a rock filling and cut hieroglyphics all over the place, telling of his wealth and social importance, and begging all future generations to regard the premises as sacred.

Some two thousand years later along comes a vandal in a cheap store suit and a cork helmet, engages Ipekak's own descendants to pry open the tomb and heave out the rock at fifteen cents per day, hauls the mummy into the daylight, and ships it by luggage van to Cairo, where it is sold to a St. Paul man for $125!

Until I talked to the dealer I had no idea that mummies were so plentiful. In some parts of Egypt people go out and dig them up just as they would dig potatoes. The prices vary greatly, somewhat depending upon the state of preservation of the party of the first part and the character of the decorations on the case, but more particularly on account of the title or historical importance of the once lamented. For instance, a Rameses or Ptolemy cannot be touched for less than $1000. A prince, a trust magnate, or a military commander brings $150; the Governor of a city or the president of a theological seminary anywhere from $60 to $75. Within the last three years perfect specimens of humourist have been offered for as low as $18, and the dealer showed me one for $7.50—probably a tourist.

At Naples, proceeding eastward, one enters the land of Talk. The French are conversational and animated, but Southern Italy begins to show the real Oriental luxuriance of gab. A Neapolitan trying to sell three cents' worth of fish will make more noise than a whole Wanamaker establishment. The most commonplace and everyday form of dialogue calls for flashing eyes, swaying body, and frantic gesticulations.

In front of a café in Naples Mr. Peasley became deeply interested in a conversation between two well-dressed men at a table near ours. At first we thought they were going to " clinch " and fight it out, but then we saw that there was no real anger exhibited, but that apparently one was describing to the other some very thrilling experience. He waved his arms,

struck at imaginary objects, made pinwheel move-
ments with his fingers, and carried on generally in a
most hysterical manner. Mr. Peasley, all worked up,
beckoned the head waiter, who had been talking to
us in English.

"Look here," he said confidentially, " I want you
to listen and tell me what those fellows are talking
about. I can't catch a word they say, but as near as
I can make out from the way they act that fellow
with the goatee is describing some new kind of tor-
pedo boat. It goes through the water at about thirty
miles an hour, having three or four screw propellers.
When it comes within striking distance of the enemy
—bang! they cut her loose and the projectile goes
whizzing to the mark, and when it meets with any
resistance there is a big explosion and everything
within a quarter of a mile is blown to flindereens.
Now, that's the plot, as near as I can follow it from
watchin' that short guy make motions. You listen
to them and tell me if I am right."

The head waiter listened and then translated to us
as follows:—"He is saying to his friend that he
slept very well last evening and got up feeling good,
but was somewhat annoyed at breakfast time because
the egg was not cooked to suit him."

" How about all these gymnastics? " asked the sur-

prised Mr. Peasley. "Why does he hop up and down,
side step and feint and wiggle his fingers and all that
monkey business?"

"Quite so," replied the head waiter. "He is describing the egg."

What a people—to take five cents worth of cheap
information and garland it with twenty dollars'
worth of Delsarte and rhetoric!

Talk is one of the few things of which there is a
superabundance in the Levant. In nearly all particulars the Arab is economical and abstemious. He
eats sparingly and cheaply, wears just enough clothing to keep from violating the municipal ordinances,
smokes conservatively, so as to get the full value of
his tobacco, and lives in a house which is furnished
with three or four primitive utensils. But when it
comes to language, he is the most reckless spend-
thrift in the world. He uses up large bales of conversation.

Suppose that three porters at a railway station
are to take a trunk from a car and put it on a truck
and wheel it out to a cab. The talk made necessary
by this simple operation would fill several pages in
the Congressional Record. All three talk incessantly,
each telling the others what to do and finding fault
because they don't do it his way. One seems to be

" He is describing the egg "

163

superintendent, the second is foreman, and the third is boss.

Endless disputes of a most vivid character rage among the donkey boys and peddlers who assemble near the hotels and lie in wait for victims. " What do they find to talk about? " is the question that comes to one every time he hears the babel of excited voices. And while we are smiling at their childish tantrums they are splitting their sides over new stories relating to that strange being from the antipodes, the barbarian with the mushroom helmet who exudes money at every pore, who keeps himself bundled in unnecessary clothes and rides out to the desert every day to stand in the baking sun and solemnly contemplate a broken column and a heap of rubbish. Truly it all depends on the point of view.

We held back the Pyramids and the Sphinx so as to make our visit to them the cap sheaf of the stay in Cairo. As for sightseeing, most of the time we just rambled up one street and down another, looking in shop windows, watching the workmen kill time with their prehistoric implements, smelling the bazaars, dodging dog carts, donkeys and camels, and having a fine time generally.

Aimless excursions are the best, after all. It is more fun to drift around a new town and rub up against the people than to deliver yourself, body and soul, over to a guide. In Egypt the guide is called a dragoman. He puts on airs and has an inside pocket bulging with testimonials from people who were so glad to get out of his clutches that they willingly perjured themselves by giving him half-hearted certificates of good character. While you are in the hands of the dragoman you feel like a dumb, driven cow. You follow the fluttering night-shirt and the tall red fez of this arch villain for hours at a time, not knowing where you are going, or why. He takes absolute charge of you, either by making specious representations or boldly assuming authority, and when you start out to visit the famous mosque of old Midullah Oblongahta or some other defunct celebrity you finish up in a junk shop for the sale of antiques, all of which are personally guaranteed by the dragoman, because he is a silent partner in the business.

In many countries, especially at times when the traveller must condense his itinerary, the guide is a necessary evil, and in Egypt he is supposed to be a sort of ornamental body guard. We found that we could wander about without being haltered and led, so we spent pleasant hours in the Mouski, which is the native shopping street, and also we went to the race meeting and saw native horses and ponies, carrying 140 to 160 pounds each, saunter around a half-mile track while a large number of English in Mardi Gras costumes drank gallons of tea and simulated a polite interest.

One afternoon we wandered into a market and a man tried to sell me a camel. Wherever we go, if a man has something he doesn't want, he tries to sell it to me, and sometimes he does it. But I refused to take the camel. I did not see how I could fold it up and secrete it so as to get it through the custom house.

Camels in the Cairo market are now steady, not literally speaking, but as regards their value. A good terra cotta camel, 55 to 60 hands high and broken to single-foot, will fetch as high as $150. The older ones—spavined, hairless, or pigeontoed—can be bought for as low as $50 each. The common or garden camel, trained to collapse like a pocket camera and carry from three to eight tons of cargo, can usually be bought at from $100 to $125.

Cairo, as a whole, was a big surprise to us. We knew that it was going to be cosmopolitan, but we were not prepared to find it so metropolitan. We had pictured it as one or two semi-European streets hedged in by a vast area of native quarter. But, unless you seek out the old parts of the town or the bazaars, each showing a distinct type of the Oriental shark, Cairo is outwardly quite modern, very attractive, and decidedly gay—that is, not real wicked gayety of the Parisian brand, but modified, winter-resort gayety, the kind that is induced by the presence of money-spending tourists. There is no hurrah night life, and gambling, which flourished here for many seasons under the skilful direction of our countryman, Mr. Pat Sheedy, has yielded to British reformatory influence.

The modern streets in Cairo, with their attractive hotels, residences, and shops, suggest a blending of Paris and the Riviera—consistent architecture, trees, palms, gardens. The streets are of boulevard width, and the houses of cheerful colouring, many of them bearing coloured frescoes in delicate shades. We who live in a country of rainfall and smoke and changing temperatures are impelled to stop and gaze in wonder at a mansion of snowy white with a pattern of pale blossoms drooping down the front of it. That style of decoration would last about twenty minutes in Chicago.

CHAPTER XIII

ALL ABOUT OUR VISIT TO THE PYRAMID
OF CHEOPS

DURING the first three days in Cairo a brilliant
and original plan of action had been outlining itself
in my mind. At last I could not keep it to myself any
longer, so I told Mr. Peasley.

"Do you know what I am going to do?" I asked.
Mr. Peasley did not.

"I am going to write up the Pyramids. I am going
to tell who built them and how long it took and how
many blocks of stone they contain. I shall have myself photographed sitting on a camel and holding
an American flag. Also, I shall describe in detail the
emotions that surge within me as I stand in the
shadow of the Sphinx and gaze up at that vast and
imperturbable expanse of face."

"It's a great scheme," said Mr. Peasley, "but
you've been scooped. They've been written up
already."

"Are you sure?"

"Yes, sir; the whole outfit of Pyramids has been

168

A VISIT TO THE PYRAMID OF CHEOPS

described in a special article by a man named Herodotus."

" How long since? "

" About 470 B. C."

He produced a guide book and proved that he was
right. All the things that I had been getting ready

" Scooped! "

to say about the Pyramids had been said by Herodotus. He had got there ahead of me—just 2376

years ahead of me. In daily newspaper competition, when some man gets his news twenty-four hours ahead of another one he is proud of his "beat" and is the hero of the office for fifteen or twenty minutes. But think of trailing along twenty-four centuries behind a Greek space writer! It took all the starch out of me.

Mr. Peasley suggested that inasmuch as considerable time had elapsed since the appearance of the first write-up, possibly the average reader would have only a dim recollection of it and accept my account as brand new stuff. But I knew better. I knew that some old subscriber, with a complete file put away in the bureau, would rise up and draw the deadly parallel on me. All I can safely do in regard to the Pyramids is touch up a few points overlooked by my predecessor.

Herodotus, by the way, had quite a time in Egypt. At that time Shepheard's Hotel was not in operation, although it must have been under way, and no round trip tickets were being issued by Cook, so Herodotus had to do his own booking and put up at a boarding house. In Memphis, which is now a fragmentary suburb of Cairo, Herodotus engaged a guide. He does not tell us what he paid, but he does give us a line on the character of the dragoman, who was full of superfluous and undesirable information, but who fell down when asked to divulge facts of real importance. This proves that the breed has not changed since 500 B. C.

The guide took Herodotus out to the Pyramids and filled him up. It is now believed that most of what Herodotus sent back was merely hearsay, but it made good reading. The Pyramids had been standing some two thousand years, and any information in regard to their origin could hardly come under the head of personal recollections. Whatever Herodotus had to say about the Pyramids is now accepted as gospel, in spite of the fact that he never saw them until twenty centuries after the last block of stone had been put in place and Cheops had taken possession of the tomb chambers. Rather late for a grand opening.

When he arrived at the Great Pyramid he stepped it off and put down the dimensions, and then he remarked to some of the natives standing around that it must have been quite a job to build a tomb of that size. They said yes; it had been a big contract, and as the work had been completed only two thousand years they were enabled to go into details. They gave Herodotus a fine lay-out of round figures. They said that one hundred thousand men had worked on the job and that the time required was thirty years— ten years to build the road and the huge incline for bringing the blocks of stone into place, and then twenty years to quarry the stone and transport it across the Nile and the valley. The stone cutters worked all the year, and during the three months' inundation, when farming was at a standstill, the entire rural population turned out, just as they would at a husking bee or a barn raising, and helped Cheops with his tomb. They did this year after year for thirty years, until they had piled up 2,300,000 blocks of stone, each containing forty cubic feet.

Herodotus discovered some large hieroglyphics on the face of the Pyramid and asked the guide for a translation. It is now supposed that the guide could not read. Anyone with education or social standing wouldn't have been a guide, even in that remote period. But this guide wanted to appear to be earning his salary and be justified in demanding a tip, so he said that the inscription told how much garlic and onions the labourers had consumed while at work on the job, and just how much these had cost. Herodotus put it all down in his notebook without batting an eye.

" How much did they spend for onions and garlic? " he asked, poising his pencil.

Herodotus put it all down—without batting an eye

The guide waited for a moment, so that his imagination could get a running start, and then he replied, " They cost 1600 talents of silver."

Now, that sum in talents is equivalent, under modern computation, to 350,000 English pounds, or $1,750,000. Think of a million dollars' worth of garlic! Try to imagine the bouquet that permeated the desert when one hundred thousand men who had been eating garlic began to call for more bricks and mortar!

Herodotus told his story and got away with it. By the time the next letter-writing traveller came along, a good many centuries later, the outer casing of the Pyramid had been stripped off and the inscription had disappeared. His story has stood because he was here ahead of the rest of us and saw the marks with his own eyes and had them translated by a ten-cent guide. But can you believe that a great monarch would devote thirty years and sacrifice thousands of lives and work the whole male population of his kingdom to skin and bones putting up a colossal sepulchre and then set aside the most valuable space on this glorious monument for telling how much onions and garlic had been fed to the help?

Marco Polo, Mark Twain, and all the other great travellers of history love to tell tall ones once in a while, but the garlic story by Herodotus will doubtless be regarded as a record performance for a long time to come.

Cheops was possibly the most successful contractor in history. It is estimated that he really did work one hundred thousand men in the building of the great Pyramid, as related by Herodotus, and that he must have devoted at least thirty years to the big undertaking. During all that time he never had a strike or even a clash with the walking delegate. The eight hour day was unknown, and no one dreamed of such a thing as an arbitration committee. All he had to do was to give orders and the entire population obeyed him. Everybody worked but Cheops. He didn't even pay salaries. It is true that in a spirit of generosity he set out a free lunch for the labourers—about $2,000,000 worth of garlic and onions. If he had tried to feed them on quail probably he would have gone broke.

Nowadays visitors go out to the Pyramids by tramcar. For some reason we had the notion, doubtless shared by many who have not been there, that to get to the Pyramids one simply rides through Cairo and out onto the flat desert. As a matter of fact, the Great Pyramid at Ghizeh, its two smaller companions and the Sphinx are on a rocky plateau five miles to the west of the city. There is a bee-line road across the lowlands. It is a wide and graded thoroughfare, set with acacia trees, and as you ride out by trolley or carriage you look up at the Pyramids, and when you are still three miles away they seem to be at least a half-mile distant. At the end of the avenue and at the foot of the hill there is a hotel, and from this point one may climb or else charter a dumb animal.

Not knowing the ropes, we engaged a carriage at 100 piastres to take us from the city out to the plateau. This is not as much as it sounds, but it is about twice the usual rate. After we struck the long road leading across the valley and saw the trolley cars gliding by and leaving us far behind, we decided to send the carriage back to the city and take to the trolley, where we would feel at home. The driver informed us that he could not return to the city, as the big bridge had been opened to permit the passing of boats, and that it would be three hours before he could drive back to town. It seems that he was right. The big bridge swings open but once a day, and then it stays open for a few hours, and the man who finds himself " bridged " must either swim or engage a boat.

It is a five minutes' climb from the end of the

drive up to the rocky plateau on which the pyramids are perched, and the ordinary tourist goes afoot. But we were pining for Oriental extravagance and new sensations, so we engaged camels. The camel allotted to me was destitute of hair, and when first discovered was in a comatose condition. His or her name was Zenobia, and the brunette in charge said that its age was either six or sixty. It sounded more like " six," but the general appearance of the animal seemed to back up the " sixty " theory. As we approached, Zenobia opened one eye and took a hard look at the party, and then made a low wailing sound which doubtless meant " More trouble for me." The venerable animal creaked at every joint as it slowly rose into the air on the instalment plan, a foot or two at a time.

We had come thousands of miles to see the Pyramids, and for the next ten minutes we were so busy hanging on to those undulating ships of the desert that we overlooked even the big Pyramid, which was spread out before us 750 feet wide and 450 feet high. Riding a camel is like sitting on a high trestle that is giving way at the joints and is about to collapse. The distance to the ground is probably ten feet, but you seem to be fifty feet in the air. As soon as we could escape from the camels we walked around and gazed in solemn silence at the Sphinx and the three Pyramids and doubtless thought all of the things that were appropriate to the time and place.

The great Pyramid of Cheops has been advertised so extensively that doubtless many people will be surprised to learn that there is a whole flock of Pyramids on this plateau along the edge of the Libyan desert. There are Pyramids to the north and Pyramids to the south, five groups in all, sixty of them, and they vary in size from a stingy little mound looking like an extinct lime kiln up to the behemoth specimen which is photographed by every Cook tourist.

Why do these Pyramids vary so greatly in size? Each was built by some royal personage as an enduring monument to his administration and the last resting place of his remains. The most eminent students of Egyptology now agree that the size of each of these Pyramids is a fair measure of the length of each king's reign. The reason that Cheops has the biggest Pyramid is that he held office longer than the others. When a king mounted the throne, if he was feeling rugged and was what an insurance company would call a " preferred risk " he would block out the foundation of a Pyramid tomb that would require, say, ten years for the building. If, at the end

178

of ten years, he was still feeling in good physical condition and confident of lasting a while longer he would widen the foundations and put on additional layers up to the summit. Labor was free and materials were cheap, and he kept everybody working on his tomb as long as he lived. Finally, when the court physicians began to warn him that his time was limited, he would begin putting on the outer coating of dressed stone and arrange for the inscriptions. The ruler who lasted only three or four years was buried in a squatty little Pyramid, which soon became hidden under the drifting sands of the desert. Cheops kept piling up the huge blocks for thirty years, and that is why his Pyramid holds the record. If Methuselah had been a Pyramid builder he would have been compelled to put up a tomb probably a mile and a half high and about eleven miles around the base. In a revolutionary South American republic the ruler would probably get no further than laying the corner stone.

We visited the pyramids. Also, we looked at the golf links, staked out across the barren sands—not to be played on, but merely to be featured in the hotel advertisement. Think of a golf course which is one huge hazard! Drive the ball in any direction and you can't play out of the sand! Forty centuries gazing down on a bow-legged tourist in fuzzy Scotch stockings!

Most of the pleasure seekers that we encountered in the neighbourhood of the Pyramids seemed to be quite elderly—some of the more sprightly as young as sixty, and from that going up to where it would be better to stop guessing. Mr. Peasley gave an explanation of their presence. He said that the dry climate of Egypt would preserve antiquities for an indefinite period.

Here they were, these male and female octogenarians, not propped up in arm chairs dividing the family silverware and arranging bequests to hospitals and libraries, but out on the blinding desert, thousands of miles from home, falling off donkeys, climbing up on camels, devouring guide books, rummaging around for time tables, kicking on the charges, and leading on the whole a life of purple strenuosity. We heard of two English women, sisters, both over seventy, who had just returned from Khartoum, from which point they had gone on a hunting expedition still further into the interior. They had to wear mosquito bags and semi-male attire, and were out in the wild country for days at a time, chasing gazelles, hyenas, and other indigenous fauna.

180

A VISIT TO THE PYRAMID OF CHEOPS

Just as I am about to conclude this treatise it occurs to me that, although I have given a wealth of useful information regarding the Pyramids, I have rather overlooked our old friend the Sphinx. I can only say in passing that it looks exactly like the printed advertisements. There is no deception about it. It is in a bad state of repair, but this is not surprising when we consider its age. Herodotus does not mention the Sphinx. It was right there at the time. In fact, it had been there fourteen hundred years when he first arrived. It seems strange that an observing traveller should have overlooked a monument sixty-six feet high, with a face nearly fourteen feet wide, a nose five feet and seven inches long, and wearing a smile that measures over seven feet! Herodotus either walked by without seeing it or else he did not think it worthy of mention. The only plausible explanation is that he was too busy figuring up the garlic statistics.

ON THE NILE

CHAPTER XIV

DASHING UP THE NILE IN COMPANY WITH MR. PEASLEY AND OTHERS

THE dream of many years has come true. We are moving (southward) up the Nile. Like busy sand flies we are flitting, almost daily, across white patches of desert to burrow into second-hand tombs and crick our necks looking up at mutilated temples.

Ten years ago not one of us had ever heard of Koti or Khnemhotep. Now we refer to them in the most casual way, as if we had roomed with them for a while. It is certainly a gay life we are leading over the cemetery circuit. Just think what rollicking fun it must be to revel day after day in sarcophagi and sepulchres, stumbling through subterranean passages and kicking up the dust of departed kings, peering down into mummy pits, also trying to stretch the imagination like a rubber band so that we may get the full significance of what is meant by 1500 B. C. People come to Egypt to cure nervous depression and then spend nine-tenths of their time hanging around tombs. Why come all the way to Egypt?

185

It is certainly a gay life

186

Why not go out to Woodlawn and run foot races from one family vault to another?

Mr. Peasley has no use for the tombs we have seen up to date. At Beni-Hassan we rode on donkeys and climbed hills for half an hour to inspect several large cubes of dim atmosphere surrounded by limestone. At Assiut we put in the best part of the afternoon toiling up to another gloomy cavern. While we stood in the main chamber of the tomb of Hapzefai (whoever he was), trying to pump up some enthusiasm, Mr. Peasley mopped his brow and declared himself.

"I'll tell you what I can do," he said. "I can take a hundred pounds of dynamite and a gang of dagoes and go anywhere along the Hudson and blow out a tomb in a week's time that will beat anything we've seen in Egypt. Then I'll hire a boy with a markin' brush to draw some one-legged men and some tall women with their heads turned the wrong way, and I'll charge six dollars to go in, and make my fortune."

The significance of the " six dollars " is that every traveller who wishes to visit the antiquities must pay a government tax of 120 piastres. He receives a " monument ticket," which he must show to the guard before entering any tomb or temple. I regret to say that the tickets are often passed along by de-

Why come all the way to Egypt?

parting travellers to those newly arrived, and as the guards do not read English, anything that looks like a monument ticket will satisfy the man at the door. At Beni-Hassan Mr. Peasley discovered, when he arrived at the tombs, that he had left his ticket at the boat. Fortunately, a fellow traveller had an extra ticket with him and Mr. Peasley had no difficulty in gaining admission to all the tombs under the name of " Miss Ella McPherson."

Before plunging into the details of our voyage, it is only fair that the indulgent reader should know how and why we came boating up the Nile. And first of all he should know something about this wonderful river. The Nile has been described one million times, at a rough guess, and yet at the risk of dealing out superfluous information I am going to insert some geography.

Total length, nearly four thousand miles. For thousands and thousands of years it has supported a swarming population along its banks, and yet until fifty years ago no one knew from whence it came. The inhabitants suspected that it came from somewhere, but they were too busy paying taxes and building pyramids to worry about scientific discoveries. For 1200 miles up stream from the delta outlet the Nile does not receive any tributary. It winds over a limestone base and through a rainless desert between high and barren tablelands. Occasionally, where there is a granite formation, the stream is narrowed and forces its way through rushing rapids, and these are known as the " cataracts." The first of these is at Assouan, about six hundred miles up stream.

Assouan has for many centuries marked the border line of Egypt proper. To the south is the land of the warlike blacks, who have been trouble-makers from the beginning of time. This First Cataract is the usual terminus of tourist travel, but those who wish to see Nubia and the Soudan board a small steamer, pass through the locks of the new dam, and go by river 210 miles to Wadi Halfa, thence by rail 576 miles to Khartoum. It is here, about thirteen hundred and fifty miles up stream, that the White and Blue Niles converge and bring down from the rainy equatorial regions the floods of muddy water which are the annual salvation of Egypt.

Ten years ago Khartoum seemed as inaccessible as the North Pole. It was headquarters for the most desperate swarm of frenzied fanatics that ever swept a region with fire and sword. They had wiped out British armies and put Gordon's head on a pole. They were in a drunken ecstasy of Mohammedan zeal, eager to fight and ready to die, and they got all that they were looking for.

It is less than eight years since Kitchener went down to call on them. Of all the cold-blooded and frozen-featured military tacticians of the inexorable school, Kitchener stands pre-eminent. General Grant in his grimmest moment was absolutely emotional and acrobatic as compared with Kitchener. He carried ice water in his veins, and his mental machinery ticked with Birmingham regularity. He did not get excited and dash into the open trap, as all the others had done. He moved slowly but relentlessly into the dread country and built a railroad as he went along. He carried everything that a British army needs— marmalade, polo ponies, Belfast ginger ale, tinned meats, pipe clay, etc.

" We cannot stampede them, because stampeding is their specialty," said Kitchener, " but I will lick them by algebra."

He did not say this, because he never said any-thing, but this is what he indicated by his calm prep-arations. He knew that the dervishes were frothing at the mouth and praying Allah to give them another chance to swim in gore, so he simply edged up to within striking distance of them and picked out his ground and waited. A kinetoscope hero would have galloped up and down the line shouting, " Up, men, and at them!" But Kitchener was not a hero. He was business manager of an abattoir. His object was not to win a great battle, but to exterminate a species. And he probably did one of the neatest jobs of house cleaning on record.

The bloodthirsty mob, led by the Khalifa, as principal maniac, charged across an open plain. Each determined dervish carried in his right hand a six foot spear, with which he hoped to do considerable damage. When he still lacked about a mile of being within poking distance of the hated infidel, the machine guns opened up and began to sweep the plain back and forth in long regular swaths, just as the sickle sweeps through the yellow grain. It was quite a handicap for the invincible children of Allah. They could not use their six foot spears on anyone a mile away, and before they could recover from the chagrin occasioned by this unexpected move on the part of the enemy, about eleven thousand of them had winged their way to eternal happiness and the others were radiating in all directions, pursued by those who wished to civilise them and bring them under British control. Those of the dervishes who escaped are supposed to be still running. At least they never came back to start another Messiah movement.

Ten years ago the Soudan was sealed to the whole world and death waited for the unbeliever who crossed the border. To-day the *table d-hôte* roams unafraid, and the illustrated post card blooms even as the rose.

The Nile of which you have read and along which are scattered the simon pure monuments of antiquity is the six hundred miles of winding river between Assouan, or First Cataract, and the sea. For the entire distance, until it spreads into a fan-shaped delta and filters into the Mediterranean, the stream is walled in by flat-topped hills of barren aspect. They are capped with limestone and carpeted about with shifting sands, and they look for all the world like the mesas of New Mexico and Arizona, for they lie baking in the same kind of clarified sunshine. This meandering hollow between the rugged hill ranges is the Valley of the Nile. Here and there the hills close in until the river banks are high and chalky cliffs. At one point the valley spreads to a width of thirty-three miles.

East and west of the hills are vast areas of desert without even a spear of vegetation except where there is a miraculous rise of water to the surface. These spots are grateful landmarks of clustered palms and are known as oases.

The Valley of the Nile would be just as bare and monotonous as an asphalt pavement were it not for the fact that once a year the Nile overflows. It has been overflowing every year for thousands of years, bringing down from the mountains of Abyssinia and the far-away regions of tropical rains a spreading volume of muddy water. Every winter, when the dwindling stream gets back into the customary bed, it has left a layer of black sediment over the inundated district. So many layers of sediment have been deposited that now the rich black soil is thirty to fifty feet deep along the river, thinning out as it meets the slope of the desert. Unlike our prairie soil of the Middle West, the Nile farms are not underlaid with clay. The Nile soil is black all the way down to limestone—a floury mineral powder of even composition. The only parts of Egypt which can be cultivated are those touched by the annual overflow. Egypt is really a ribbon of alluvial soil following the stream on either side. The tourist standing on the top deck of a Nile steamer can see both east and west the raw and broken edges of the desert.

The entire population lives on the river, literally and figuratively. Dark-robed women come down to the stream in endless processions to fill their water jars, and it seems that about every forty feet or so all the way up from Cairo the industrious fellah is lifting water up the bank and irrigating his little field with the same old-fashioned sweep and bucket arrangement that was in use when Joseph came over to Egypt and attracted the attention of Potiphar's wife. The Egyptian farmer is called a fellah. The clothing that he wears would wad a gun—that is, a rifle, not a shotgun. He puts in at least fourteen hours a day and his pay is from ten to fifteen cents. Mr. Peasley told a tourist the other day that the song "He's a jolly good fellah" originated in Egypt during the time of the Ptolemies. This is a sample of the kind of idiotic observation that is supposed to enliven a so-called pleasure trip.

But let us get back to the river, for in Egypt one must get back to the river at least once every twenty minutes. The Nile is Egypt and Egypt is the Nile. All this description may sound like a few pages from the trusty red guide book, and yet the word "Egypt" will have no meaning to the reader who does not get a clear panoramic vision of this wonderfully slim-waisted country. Nearly six hundred miles long and yet containing only twelve thousand five hundred square miles—about the size of Maryland.

The strip of black land which yields the plentiful crops is nowhere more than ten miles wide, a mere fringe of fertility weaving along through dryness and desolation. Anywhere along the river if you will climb to the rocky plateau, you will see the slow moving river, probably a half-mile wide, as a glassy thread on which are strung fields of living green, bordered by the dreary uplifts of desert. The traveller who goes by boat from Cairo to Assouan sees all of Egypt. The cities and temples and tombs of olden times were perched on the high spots or planted in the bare hills, so as to be safe from the annual rise of waters. Anything worth seeing in the whole country is within an easy donkey ride of the river bank. The river is the only artery of travel. There is a railway, but it follows the river all the way up to Assouan.

It would seem that the country was especially laid out and punctuated with " sights " for the convenience of the modern traveller, for the visitor who goes up the Nile and stops off at the right spots can do a clean job of sight seeing without doubling on his tracks.

Until a few years age the tourist going up the Nile had to take a dahabeah. This sounds like the name of a disease, but it is really a big, roomy, flat-bottomed sailboat. The dahabeah moves only when the wind is in the right direction, and to go from Cairo to Assouan requires the greater part of a lifetime. Those travellers who have money to burn and who are content to settle down to many weeks of rest and indolence charter the private dahabeahs. When a traveller goes aboard a dahabeah he tears up the calendar and lets his watch run down. Those who have more money and are in a hurry use the private steam dahabeahs.

A majority of travellers go by passenger boats. The tourist steamers devote three weeks to a loafing voyage up to Assouan and back, with daily excursions to the graveyards and ruins. The express steamers, carrying freight and native passengers, take less time for the round trip, as they skip some of the less interesting antiquities. We took an express steamer, thereby missing many of the tombs and temples, but still getting enough of them to last us for the next hundred years or so.

Our steamer is a frail affair, double decked and of no draught worth mentioning. It resembles the old style of Missouri River boat, built to run on a heavy dew. There are thirty passengers, who devote most of their time to lolling on deck waiting for the next meal. Mud banks, natives hoisting water, green fields stretching away to the bald range of hills, 'dobe huts, spindly palms, now and then a solemn

197

row of camels, always several donkeys and goats in evidence, every few miles the tall stack of a sugar mill, perpetual sunshine—it is monotonous travel, and yet there is continually something doing along the banks, and the traveller cannot get away from

Lying back to watch others work

that feeling of satisfaction which results from lying back to watch other people work.

And the sunsets! You cannot estimate the real dignity and artistic value of a camel until you see him or her silhouetted against a sky of molten gold just at twilight. I have made two or three attempts to describe the glory of a sunset in the desert, but I find myself as helpless as Mr. Peasley, who, after gazing for five minutes at the flaming horizon can only murmur a low but reverent " Gosh! "

It may interest the reader to hear what Baedeker has to say on the subject. Baedeker says (p. 216) " The sunsets are very fine." That's what I like about Baedeker. He doesn't fuss over a lot of words and tack on superfluous adjectives. As soon as he has imparted the necessary information in a trim and concise manner he moves on to the next subject.

I am sending herewith two sketches which show the beauty and variety of landscape to which we are treated every day. View No. 1 is most characteristic. We see before us the rippling Nile and beyond it the sheer river bank of black dirt. Then the field of waving grain, in the distance the range of hills, and over all a dazzling sunshine.

No. 2 is more varied. Again we have the river, the mud bank, and the growing crops, together with the distant hills, behind which the sun is silently sinking. In the foreground at the left is a majestic palm. The structure at the right is a native house and will indicate something of the simple life of the agricul-

199

turist. The complicated device on the river bank at stage centre is the shadouf, used for lifting water from the stream. The cavernous opening in the distant hill (marked X in the drawing) is the entrance to a rock tomb. By studying this picture the reader

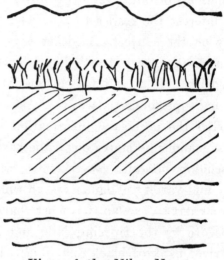

View of the Nile—No. 1

may get a very fair understanding of the architectural splendour of these ancient seuplchres.

Travelling on the Nile has two reliable features to commend it. The weather is always fair and the native population constantly enlivens the picture, for the lower river is crowded with sails and every inch along the banks is under cultivation. Also, the Nile

has some surprises in store. Two definite delusions
are soon shattered.

Delusion No. 1.—HEAT. It is not always warm
in Egypt. In the middle of the day, out of the wind

View of the Nile—No. 2

and on the desert, it may work up to a good summery
temperature at this season, but in the shade it is cool,
and as soon as the sun has set, a bracing autumnal
chill comes into the air and the heavy overcoat is
needed. The north wind can be very chiselly at
times. If coming to Egypt, bring your flannels
along.

Delusion No. 2.—CROCODILES. There are no crocodiles in the Nile. We have always supposed that the bank of the river was polka-dotted with these monsters, lying in wait for small, dark children. It is said that two thousand years ago the Nile was bordered with papyrus reeds or bullrushes, within the tangles of which lurked hippopotami, crocodiles, dragomans, and other reptiles, but the animals have disappeared, and so has the river vegetation. The other day we visited the island on which Pharaoh's daughter discovered little Moses. The island is still there, but there isn't a bullrush within a mile of it.

One of the penalties of travel is to have old and settled beliefs uprooted. For instance, there are no Maltese cats in Malta, no Venetian blinds in Venice, no Roman punch in Rome. If you want Neapolitan ice cream in Naples you must send out for it. You may walk about all day in Bologna without seeing a pound of Bologna sausage. Egyptian cigarettes are known throughout the world, and yet no tobacco is grown in Egypt. Go to Manhattan Beach and everybody is drinking Martinis. Truly, the stereotyped labels are deceptive.

CHAPTER XV

DAY BY DAY ON THE DROWSY NILE. WITH SOMETHING ABOUT THE WONDERFUL HASSIM

WHILE we were in London we dined one evening at a gorgeous hotel with a Mr. Brewster, of Connecticut. After dinner, Mr. Peasley told the waiter to bring some " good cigars." Mr. Peasley resides in Iowa, where it is customary to stroll down to the drug store after supper and buy a couple of Lottie Lees, which are so good that the druggist cannot afford to give six for a quarter. Not being familiar with the favourite brands of London, he called on Mr. Brewster to name the cigar of his choice, and Mr. Brewster said he was very fond of the Corona del Matadora, or something like that, because the entire crop in Cuba was taken over by a London dealer, and they could not be obtained in New York for love or money. The waiter brought what appeared to be a very superior article of stogie, and after they had been passed around, Mr. Peasley put several into his pockets, as we were going to a music hall, and Mr. Peasley had learned that tobacco acted as a sedative and helped one to remain calm while listening to British jokes.

" How much? " he asked.

" Three and six," replied the waiter.

" Each," said the waiter

Mr. Peasley handed him three and six.

" Each," said the waiter.

Mr. Peasley swallowed something and his eyes leaned from their sockets, but he said nothing. He handed over two sovereigns, and the change that came back to him was almost sufficient for the waiter's tip. There was a brief silence and then Mr. Peasley said:—" Three shillings is seventy-five cents —seventy-five and twelve make eighty-seven."

Another silence.

" Eighty-seven cents," sighed Mr. Peasley. " Three bushels of oats for a cigar!"

When Mr. Brewster crossed our trail in Egypt and became our fellow passenger on a Nile steamer Mr. Peasley remembered him and longed for a chance to get even.

Our friend from Connecticut was wearing a large canopy helmet—the kind that makes a short man look like a walking piano-stool. We were wearing the same outlandish style of headgear and for some reason or other, no person being responsible for what he does when he is away from home, Mr. Peasley had his name boldly marked in Arabic on the front of his helmet. It didn't look like anything, but it was real Arabic and said his name was Peasley and that he came from Iowa and he was very proud of it. He urged Mr. Brewster to have his helmet marked in a similar way.

" I hardly like the idea of wearing my name on my hat," said the man from Connecticut.

" But when you get home and hang the thing up in your den with the Navajo blankets and swords and other curios, think what a fine souvenir it will be," urged Mr. Peasley.

Mr. Brewster finally consented and Mr. Peasley took the helmet to the head steward, who was a native, and in a few minutes he brought it back magnificently lettered all over the front. It surely did look Oriental and decorative and Mr. Brewster was grateful when he saw how beautifully his name and New England address showed up in Arabic.

That afternoon we landed at Assiut, which is head-quarters for a most wolfish assortment of guides, street peddlers, and hold-up men who work in the bazaars. Most of them are Copts and claim to be good Christians, but we did not feel impelled to throw up our hats on that account. When they bore down upon us and started to wrestle with us we could hardly distinguish any difference between them and the ordinary heathen.

From the moment that we landed, Mr. Brewster of Connecticut attracted more attention than any other person in the party. Four guides laid hold of him at the same moment and declined to let go. Later on, in the bazaar, every dealer who sighted him gave a glad guttural cry and tried to drag him

" *Rich American—easy mark* "

into one of the stuffy little shops. The arrival of an ordinary tourist is calculated to agitate a bazaar, but when Mr. Brewster appeared the general effect was the same as when the raw meat is carried into the zoo. He was pulled and hauled and for the whole length of the winding bazaar his way was blocked by frantic villains in white gowns and huge turbans, who dangled tawdry merchandise in front of him and begged him to make an offer. Mr. Brewster was a good deal amazed, and we were more or less puzzled until we came back to the boat and Mr. Peasley confessed that the Arabic characters boldly displayed on Mr. Brewster's helmet did not stand for his name and address at all, but meant, as nearly as could be translated, " Rich American—Easy Mark."

Poor Mr. Brewster! At the present writing he is still wearing that bold label, wandering in and out of shops and around hotels, inviting the attacks of guides, donkey boys, servants, and peddlers. It seemed a rather low-down trick, but Mr. Peasley said that probably it would flatter Mr. Brewster to learn that anyone from Connecticut could attract so much attention in a foreign country.

Arabic is surely a weird excuse for a language. In its written form it looks like the bird-track illustrations in one of Thompson Seton Thompson's books, and instead of reading it from left to right you begin at the tail end of a sentence and back up all the way. In reading an Arabic novel you turn to the end of the book and read the last chapter first, and if it develops that the fellow marries the girl, naturally that saves a lot of trouble. In its right to left character the Arabic is somewhat like the Hebrew or Lower Broadway language, which also begins at the leaving-off place. This fact reminded a New York man of a story. He said that in one of the east side Assembly districts of New York city a large body of Yiddish voters, recently arrived in the land of the somewhat free and the home of the more or less brave, had been rounded up very carefully by the Tammany workers. The voters were not familiar with the workings of the Australian ballot system, and had to be instructed by the Tammany ward heelers, who said:—" All you have to do is to put a cross mark in the circle at the top of the first column, see? " That seemed simple enough, so the voters went into the booths and marked the first —that is, the right hand—column, and elected the Prohibition candidate.

The Arabic language, when spoken, sounds very much like an agitated person trying to dislodge a fish bone. It is one of the most unmusical tongues

in the world and offers no tempting inducements to
the student, yet Mr. Peasley actually bought one
of those " Arabic at a Glance " books and started
to learn some of the more useful sentences. He said
that if he could get Arabic down pat he would pass
as a native and be enabled to buy things at about
half price. After two days of hard study he attempted a conversation with a military policeman
standing on the river bank at Dendera. Mr. Peasley
strolled up to him, careless like, and said, " Ana
awez arabiyet kwayesset min shan arookh el balad."
That was supposed to mean, " I want a first-class
carriage for driving in the town." The stalwart
soldier gazed at Mr. Peasley with a most bewildered
look in his jet black eyes and then began to edge
away.

" Hold on," said Mr. Peasley. " How about hal
yel zamna ghafar yerafegua bill tareeg? "

Mr. Peasley thought he was asking, " Shall we
require a guide or an escort in this town? "

The soldier beckoned to us to come over and help
him out.

" Tell him, please, that I am educate at the Presbyterian Mission," said he. " I speak only English and
Arabic."

We questioned him later and learned that he took

THE WONDERFUL HASSIM

Mr. Peasley to be a Russian. This one little experience rather discouraged our travelling companion.
He said it was foolish to waste important dialogue

*" How about hal yel zamna ghafar yerafegua
bill tareeg? "*

on a lot of benighted ignorami who did not know their
own language.

As a matter of fact, English carries the tourist
everywhere in Egypt. The American Mission School,

211

supported by the Presbyterians, is a proud local institution in each good-sized town. At every landing along the river small boys from the mission schools would come down to the boat to ask for English books. These requests were such a welcome variation from the everlasting howl for " baksheesh " that the over-generous passengers soon gave away all the reading matter on board and had nothing left for themselves except Baedekers and time tables. I saw a silver-haired old lady from Philadelphia give to a coal-black and half-naked child of eight a volume of Browning's poems in paper cover. The dusky infant clasped the book to his bare bosom and shouted his thanks as the boat headed up stream, and the old lady was so gratified and happy that she stood looking at him with tear-dimmed eyes and never gave a thought as to what might happen to his intellect. At one town, just as we were casting off, I threw an American magazine to a handsome little tike who had been asking for English literature. It fell on the dock, and twenty small boys began fighting for it and tearing it to pieces. I never saw such a thirst for advertising matter.

Our voyage from Cairo to Luxor was punctuated with so many new experiences that possibly it would

be better to take them in order. Egypt is the land
of leisurely travel. If you look at the map the distance from Cairo to Luxor seems only a good hop,
skip, and jump. It is 458 miles by rail and the
lightning express does it in fifteen hours, the same
being considered a record performance. Our boat
left Cairo one Friday afternoon and arrived at Luxor
the following Thursday morning. We chugged
slowly against the current all the way, tying up every
night and getting away before daybreak next morning. Several times we changed pilots. The Nile
pilot is usually a grizzled old sheikh with the doubt-
ful combination of a department store spring overcoat and a red fez. He stands at the wheel bossing
the crew while the ostensible captain or manager,
who is a budding European in a neat uniform, has
nothing much to do except circulate on the upper
deck and pour tea for a little cluster of intellectual
giantesses from England. Two sailors stand well
forward on the lower deck, one on each side, jabbing
at the river with poles in order to get the depth of
the channel. If the boat runs into water less than
six inches deep they become alarmed and start to
yelp. Occasionally the gallant craft strikes a bar
and comes to a tired pause, whereupon all the passengers say "Mgh!" and lurch out of their camp

stools. Then there is a little welcome excitement and the natives of the crew run around in circles and call upon Allah for temporary assistance. With much grunting, both by the boat and the men at the poles, the good Hatasoo backs out of the mud and takes a fresh start, zigzagging through the shallows until deep water is found—that is, a depth of anywhere from three to four feet. The Nile is just as finical and unreliable as a Missouri or Mississippi, the tortuous channel constantly shifting, and the pilot needs to be an expert with a memory like an encyclopaedia. Fortunately there are no snags. Wood is about the most precious commodity in Egypt, and all the snags were fished out and utilised some two thousand years before we happened along. Although our voyage lasted five full days we went ashore only three times. As I have already explained, the traveller need not leave the Nile steamer in order to see nearly everything that is happening in Egypt. Leaving Cairo late on Friday afternoon, we made two stops on Saturday to discharge freight and take on natives. Many of the women came aboard closely veiled and were at once secreted in a canvas compartment on the lower deck. These precautions seemed to be needless. Two adjectives will best describe the pride of the harem—shabby and flabby. Unless you wish to lose all enthusiasm for the Arabian Nights, keep away from Egypt.

Sunday.—Arriving at Beni Hassan at ten o'clock we went ashore and climbed on midget donkeys and rode away to explore the rock tombs. Beni Hassan has been for several centuries the home of an obstreperous breed of cutthroats. Repeated attempts have been made to exterminate or scatter the tribe, but it is still in existence, although somewhat subdued. The government keeps a guard of soldiers at the town, and when we landed we found ourselves surrounded by the military, while the natives stood back of the dead-line and gazed at us hungrily. There we began to get close glimpses of the domestic life of the plain people.

A mud wall enclosure with a hut at one end. Within this squalid pen, women in bedraggled black gowns, children in semi-attire and closely attended by swarms of flies, two or three emaciated goats, a few chickens, and a somnolent burro. At present the live stock and the Egyptians live on terms of democratic equality, but since the English have introduced the Society for the Prevention of Cruelty to Animals it is hoped that the situation will be remedied.

On Monday, at two o'clock, we landed at Assiut,

after passing through the locks of the first big
barrage or dam built under British direction and
intended to regulate the water level of the lower
Nile and the delta during the dry season. Assiut is
a big town with some showy buildings, an attractive
bazaar, and a guide who represents the thirty-third
degree of scoundrelism. His name is Hassim. If you
should visit Assiut and wish to become acquainted
with the very pink and flower of villainy, hunt up
Hassim. Perhaps it will be unnecessary to hunt him
up. He will be waiting for you, just as he was waiting for us. When we went ashore we were attacked
by a flying wedge of donkey boys and carriage drivers, all shrieking like demons and kicking up such
clouds of dust as can be found only in a country
where the showers are a century apart. By striking
out right and left we held off our assailants and succeeded in boarding a rickety victoria. When we
escaped from the clamour and the clouds of dust and
took our bearings Hassim was on the box alongside
of the driver. He had attached himself to us on his
own invitation and we are glad that he did so, for
he proved to be a rascal of such inventive fancy and
such unusual methods of attack that our natural
resentment was fairly lost in admiration. He was tall
and lean, with a stern and military countenance and

216

one eye set at an angle. His manner was imperious and from the moment when he fastened himself upon us he was in absolute charge of the expedition.

" Fear not," he said, holding up his hand impressively, " I shall protect you. You shall see the rock tombs and the grand view of the valley and the great bazaar of Assiut and no one shall do you harm, for I am Hassim, son of Abdalla."

This had a most assuring sound, so we made no resistance. For several hours he marched ahead of us, proclaiming our social importance and ordering people out of the way, and every ten minutes he led us into some carefully concealed trap and tried to separate us from our piasters. All the time he went through the motions of defending our interests and fighting back those who would defraud us. For instance, in the bazaar. In a thoughtless moment I had said that I wished to purchase an ebony walking-stick. He led us to a dealer in walking-sticks, and here the following drama was played for our benefit:—

Hassim (to dealer)—This distinguished gentleman wishes to buy an ebony walking-stick. Show him your best goods and let the price be fair or never more shall I bring customers to your vile shop. (To the crowd jostling in upon us)—Stand back! Do not crowd upon the honourable gentlemen from America.

Dealer (showing an ebony stick with a badly carved handle of bone, supposed to be ivory)—Ah, see! Yes! Verra good stick! Is it not? Verra cheap.

I (looking at it coldly and shaking my head as if in disapproval)—How much?

Dealer—Verra cheap—only twenty shilling.

Hassim—Wha-a-t! (He rushes upon the dealer, smites him on the chest with his open hand and then tries to choke him). Oh, dog! Oh, unclean animal! Twenty shilling! (To us) Come! Let us go away. He is bad man. Come!

Dealer (entreatingly)—You make me offer. How much you give?

Hassim—Oh, child of darkness! Oh, crawling crocodile! You are trying to cheat the high-born visitors.

Dealer (cringingly)—How much you give?

Hassim (to me)—Come, I will speak with you alone. (He leads me away from the crowd and talks to me in a husky whisper.) This man is bad man. Do not pay him twenty bob. No one is looking. You slip the money to me and I will buy it for fifteen.

Now, fifteen shillings is $3.75 in real money, and the stick is worth a dollar at the most extravagant valuation, so I say to Hassim, " Are you in on this? "

He does not understand, but he looks at me as if hurt or disappointed, and then says, " I try to get it for ten. Wait here."

Then I catch him by the slack of the blue gown and say that I will not give ten. I authorise him to offer fifteen piasters—seventy-five cents. He says it will be useless to offer such a small sum, as the ivory comes from the elephant and hunters must search many days to find the elephant and then carry the tusk forty-seven thousand miles across the burning desert to sell it to the dealer in Assiut. So I tell him to stand back and I will negotiate in my own behalf. So I break through the crowd and offer three shillings. Derisive laughter by the dealer, the crowd assisting. I offer four shillings. The dealer says, " I am a ruined man, but no matter—take it along for eight." Then Hassim elbows his way back to the scene of trouble and helps to complicate matters. He curses the dealer in Arabic and says to me in a side whisper that he has succeeded in buying the stick for seven shillings. I offer five. To make a long story short, after using up $8 worth of time and $52 worth of vocal energy, I buy the stick for six shillings, and when I return to the boat the head steward exhibits one just like it which he bought for two.

This farcical " grand stand " play was repeated every time we stopped to purchase some trifling specimen of native junk. One of the best performances of the afternoon involved a mysterious trip up a narrow alley and into a tumbledown house, where Hassim exhibited to us four squalling infants, attended by many flies and richly encrusted with the soil of their native land. Although all four of the children seemed to be of about the same age, he assured us that they belonged to him, and we, being unfamiliar with the customs of Egypt, were not prepared to contradict him. He said it was customary for visitors to give a small present to each of the children, or, better still, we could give the money to him and he would hand it to them later.

We shall remember Hassim. He surrounded his cheap trickeries with such a glamour of Oriental ceremony and played his part with such a terrific show of earnestness that he made the afternoon wholly enjoyable. When we arrived at the landing he and the driver had a verbal war, and then he took me aside for another heart to heart talk.

" The driver is a child of evil," said he. " I tremble with rage! He is demanding fifty piasters.

Do not pay him fifty. Give the money to me and I will say to him, ' Take forty or nothing '! "

The driver's legal fare was twenty piasters. Finally we paid him twenty-five. Everybody was satisfied. Then we paid Hassim for his services and sent presents to his four simultaneous children, and the last we saw of him he was making a bee-line for the bazaar to collect his commissions.

The decorative tail piece to this chapter is my name in Arabic.

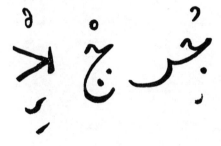

IN LUXOR

CHAPTER XVI

THE MOHAMMEDAN FLY AND OTHER CREA-
TURES LIVING ALONG THE NILE

EGYPTIAN civilisation is supposed to be station-
ary, except in the larger cities. The fellahin scratch
the rich alluvial soil with the same kind of clumsy
wooden plough that was used when Marc Antony
came down from Rome on a business trip and got all
snarled up with Cleopatra. They live in the same type
of snug mud hut—about the size of a lower berth.
They lift the water from the Nile by exactly the
same wooden sweep that was in vogue when Cheops
began work on the Pyramids. It may be remarked,
en passant, that the fellahin are the farmers of
Egypt. I might have said " farmers " in the first
place, but what is the use of spending a month in
a place and paying large hotel bills if one cannot
pick up words of the fellahin description to parade
up and down in front of his friends and cause them
to feel ignorant and untravelled? The *en passant*,
which is tucked in so neatly above, I found in Paris.
It means " under your hat," or something like that.

It is impossible to translate these French phrases without sacrificing some of the piquant significance of the original. For instance, " string beans " can never be *haricots vert*. They may look the same and taste the same, but when they are both on the bill, me for the *haricots vert* every time.

To resume:—The outlying districts of Egypt are supposed to be absolutely nonprogressive. This is a mistake. While driving out from Assiut to visit another cheerful group of tombs we came upon a large gang of workmen engaged in improving the road. As soon as the carriage ahead of ours struck the improved road it turned turtle, and for a moment the air was full of jumping tourists. Our conveyance started over the improved section, but mired down, so we got out and walked until we came to an unimproved road, and then we jumped in and sped merrily on our way. I stopped for several minutes to watch the men at work, and I was deeply impressed by the fact that here in this heathen land, where they had no normal schools or farmers' institutes to guide them, no agricultural weeklies to beacon them out of the darkness, the simple children of the Orient were " improving " the roads just as I had seen them improved during my boyhood days in Indiana. In other words, they were scooping dirt out of the ditch on either side and dumping it in tall, unsurmountable hillocks right in the middle of the roadway. The most hydrocephalous township supervisor in the whole Middle West could not have done a more imbecilic job.

In Indiana every voter is required to "work the roads" or pay a road tax. Of late years, under intelligent direction, the highways have been vastly improved, but there was a time when "working the roads" was a large joke. To avoid paying the tax the farmer would have to go out with a team and do something to a public highway. Usually he selected a road which he would not traverse in going to town, and he would plough it up and "scrape" it into hollows and leave it looking like a sample of the Bad Lands of Montana. As soon as the tax was "worked out" he discontinued the improvement. After two or three days of "working," a fairly bad road could be made altogether impassable. If I were a military commander and had to execute a retreat and cut off any pursuit by a superior force I would have a corps of flat-headed township supervisors bring up the rear and "work" the roads.

It was in this same town of Assiut that we visited one of the greatest bazaars in Egypt. We had heard about this bazaar every day since landing. The

Working out his taxes and improving the roads

traveller who had been up the Nile and who had come back to Cairo, sunbaked and full of the patronising airs of the veteran, invariably said, " By the way, when you are in Assiut you must see the bazaar." He might as well have said, " When you are in Washington be sure to take a look at the Washington Monument."

" Bazaar " has a seductive, Far Eastern sound, the same as " mosque." It is much luckier to shut your eyes and think of a mosque than to actually see a deserted lime kiln with an upturned sugar bowl on top of it. The same for " bazaar," only it goes double. A bazaar is a cosey corner gone wrong. If you will take the long corridor of an American second-class hotel, tear off the roof and substitute a canopy of tattered rag carpets, cover the walls with the imitation merchandise of a five and ten cent store, kick up a choking dust, turn loose twenty or thirty ripe odours and then have one hundred and fifty coffee-coloured lunatics all begin talking at the same time, you will have a rather tame imitation of the genuine Oriental bazaar as made famous in song and story. The crude articles sold in these bazaars, if displayed in the windows of a department store in America, would attract no attention whatever, but the tourist, as soon as he has had a touch of the Egyptian sun, seems to become easy and irresponsible, and he wants to bargain for everything in sight. It is a kind of temporary mania, known as curiosis, and is closely allied to the widely prevalent souveniria, or post card fever, which attacks even the young and innocent.

The intelligent reader may have noticed that now and then I have referred to the dust of Egypt. Egypt makes all the other dusty spots on earth seem dank and waterlogged. We asked truthful Hassim, our guide at Assiut, if there had been any rainfall lately. He said that about five years ago there had been a light shower, and during one of the Ptolemy administrations there had been a regular old drencher. The Ptolemy family occupied the throne about two thousand years ago. At home, take it in the dog days, if we have no rain for two weeks and the crick dries up, all the local apostles of gloom and advance agents of adversity clot themselves together in front of the Post Office and begin pronouncing funeral orations over the corn crop. Fourteen days without rain and the whole country is on the toboggan, headed straight for bankruptcy. Yet here in Egypt, where they haven't experienced a really wet rain for twenty centuries, the people go about cheerfully, and there is no complaint regarding Providence.

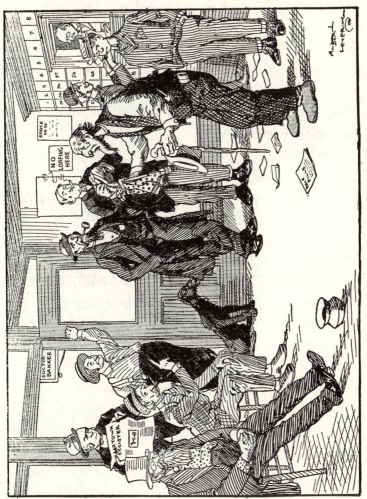

The whole country is on the toboggan

But what an unsatisfactory hang-out for the weather shark! In Egypt the oldest inhabitant never gets up in the morning and says, " I'm satisfied we're going to have rain to-day, because my rheumatiz bothered me all night." There is no need of looking for rings around the moon. You never hear anyone say, " It looks a little black in the north, but I think it'll blow around, because the wind is in the wrong direction." Every morning the sun rolls up in silvery splendour and surveys the same old parched landscape, with the strip of irrigated green, and after a leisurely and monotonous day sinks through a golden glow into the far-stretching desert. No one is looking for rain or hoping for it. When it comes it is regarded as a calamity. It washes down the mud huts, collects in pools and makes breeding spots for microbes and leaks through hotel roofs, so that tourists have to carry umbrellas in going to the dining-room. In March of this year there was a heavy rainfall around Assouan, extending as far north as Luxor, and when we came along, a few weeks later, the natives were still bewailing the visitation of Allah's wrath.

The extreme dryness of the air in Egypt causes the visiting microbe to feel like an alien. It becomes enervated and discouraged, incapable of initiating any new and fashionable epidemics. This same air, however, seems to have a tonic effect on the flea. In no other clime is he so enterprising, so full of restless energy, so given to unexpected achievements. During a dull season, if there is a short supply of tourists, he associates with the natives. He prefers the tourist, but come what may, he is never idle. The bacillus, on the other hand, has circumscribed opportunities. Inasmuch as the entire population of the country lives along the river one might suppose that harmful germs would be bred and disseminated by the billion. Yet both natives and visitors drink from the river with impunity. " The sweet water of the Nile " it is called and even the most apprehensive travellers learn to take it after putting in about twenty drops of Scotch, so as to benumb the bacilli, if any should be present. There is an explanation of the micro-organism's failure to do very much harm in Egypt. If a bacillus living anywhere along the Nile starts for a ramble on shore he is sunstruck, and falls helpless in the sand. If he sticks to the water the monotony of travel begins to wear upon him, and after about seven miles he dies of *ennui.*

If Egypt is a happy hunting ground for the flea it is likewise a paradise for the fly. If I had to be something in Egypt I should prefer to be a Mohammedan fly. This little creature, which in most countries is hounded and persecuted and openly regarded as a pest, is treated with consideration in Egypt—humoured, petted, indulged, actually spoiled. In the U. S. A. a fly is almost as unpopular as the millionaire.

In the U. S. A. the fly is almost as unpopular as a millionaire

He is wary, fretful, and suspicious, because he knows that all humanity is joined in a conspiracy to put him out of business. If he strolls up to a pool of water, temptingly set forth in a white bowl, he finds himself a few minutes later writhing in cramps and full of corrosive sublimate. He sees what appears to be a tempting luncheon of sweets and when he starts in to serve himself he discovers that he is caught and held by the treacherous " tanglefoot " mixture. He sees a sign, " This way to the dining-room," and after passing through a long corridor he lands in a wire trap from which there is no escape. If he alights on a bald head and trys to use it as a rink somebody strikes at him and calls him names.

It is all different in Egypt. The greatest indignity that a Mohammedan ever offers a fly is to give him a gentle shove and request him to move on. It is contrary to the religious teachings to kill or even cripple this diminutive household companion. The belief in the transmigration of souls seems to prevail everywhere in the mystical East, and perhaps the fly that follows and nags you all afternoon may harbour the spiritual essence of a former head waiter or a bey or some other dignitary. When the flies assemble in large numbers around the various aper- tures of a baby's face, the child, obeying an instinct of self-defence, tries to " spat " them and drive them away. But the mother restrains the infant by hold- ing its hands and the flies give themselves over to unmolested enjoyment. The older children have learned their lesson and seldom make any effort to brush away the flies which loiter all over their bright young features. This is not a pleasant thing to talk about, but inasmuch as the fly is omnipresent during a trip up the Nile and this friendly understanding between the fly and the native is constantly under the traveller's observation, a description of Egypt would be sadly incomplete without a chapter on the fly.

Having been a privileged class for many generations, the flies are impudent and familiar to a degree. When the white unbeliever, with no conscientious scruples against murder, comes up the river, they swarm about him and buzz into his ears, "Welcome to our city." Then when he begins sparring with them and using sulphurous language, they gather about him in augmented numbers and dodge when he strikes and side step when he slaps himself and seem to think that he is trying to teach them some new kind of a "tag" game. The Mohammedan fly cannot by any effort of the imagination bring himself to believe that a human being would wilfully injure him. This feeling of overconfidence in mankind breeds carelessness, and during the open season for tourists many of them are laid low. Mr. Peasley said that if there was anything in the transmigration theory, he figured that he had massacred a regiment of soldiers, several boards of directors, a high school and an insane asylum. The mortalities during the tourist season do not seem to lower the visible supply or in any way discourage the surviving millions.

When we started up the river a peddler came to the boat and offered us some small fly brooms. They are very much like the brush used by the apprentice in a blacksmith shop to protect the horse that is being shod. The brush part is made of split palm leaves or horsehair and the handle is decorated with beadwork. The idea of a person sitting about and whisking himself with this ornamental duster struck us as being most unusual, not to say idiotic. Before we travelled far up the Nile we had joined the grand army of whiskers. The fly broom is essential. It is needed every eight seconds. At Luxor we went out to see a gymkhana under the auspices of the Luxor Sporting Club and every one of the two hundred spectators sat there wearily slapping himself about the head with the tufted fly brush while looking at the races.

The Luxor Sporting Club is not as dangerous as it sounds. The presiding judge of the races was a minister of the gospel and the receipts were given to local charities. A gymkhana is the last resort of a colony shut off from the metropolitan forms of amusement, and yet it can be made the source of much hilarious fun. Nothing could have been more frivolous than the programme at Luxor, and yet the British spectators seldom gave way to mirth. Doubtless they were laughing inwardly. Several ponderous committees had charge of the arrangements and attended to them with due solemnity.

First there was a race between native water-carriers, distance about three hundred yards, and each contestant carrying a goat skin filled with water. Then there was a donkey boys' race, each rider being required to ride backward. This enabled him to encourage his mount by twisting the tail. In the donkey race for ladies several of the contestants fell off gracefully and were carried to the refreshment booth, where they revived on tea. The "affinity race" was an interesting feature. The contestants rode their donkeys in pairs, a gentleman and a lady holding a long ribbon between them. They were required to gallop about two hundred yards, turn a post, and return to the starting point without letting go of the ribbon. By far the most exciting features of the programme were the camel and buffalo races. These animals have associated with the hysterical

238

natives so long that they have lost all of their natural horse sense and are quite daft and irresponsible. At the word " Go! " instead of running down the course, they would snort madly and start off in all directions. If any of them finished under the wire it was by mere chance and not because of any guiding intelligence. One demented water buffalo turned and ran at right angles to the course. The last we saw of him he was disappearing over a hill toward the setting sun, with the native jockey riding on all parts of the upper deck, from the horns back to the tail.

The gymkhana is intended to provide an afternoon of undiluted nonsense, and for the benefit of those who find reason tottering on her throne and who don't care what they do as long as they enjoy themselves, I shall append a few sample competitions from an Egyptian programme and suggest that they be tried in America.

Bucket Contest—Competitors to gallop past three buckets, throwing a potato into each bucket. Marks to be given for pace. Best of two runs.

Hat Trimming Competition—Gentleman to ride to lady with parcel containing hat and trimmings. Lady to trim hat and gentleman to return to the winning post wearing hat.

Dak Race—Competitors to drive at the trot about one-half mile, unharness and saddle same pony and ride 200 yards, returning to the winning post.

Housekeeping Stakes—Gentleman on side saddle to ride to lady and give her envelope containing an addition sum. Lady to open envelope, add up this sum and return it to gentleman. First past the post with correct sum wins.

Needle Threading Competition—Lady carries needle and thread 100 yards to gentleman partner. He threads the needle and returns it to lady. First past the post with needle properly threaded wins.

Egg Carrying Competition for Ladies—Each lady carries an egg in an ordinary teaspoon for a distance of about fifty yards. If egg is dropped it must be recovered with the spoon and must not be touched with the hands. First past the post with unbroken egg wins.

There are many other contests which tax the intellect in a similar manner, but possibly the foregoing will be sufficient to provide a fairly demoralising afternoon. Of course, in America it is impossible to secure the real Levantine donkey. In Egypt the donkey takes the place of the motor car, the trolley, the hansom, and the bicycle. In size he ranges from an average goat to a full grown St. Bernard.

Ordinarily he is headstrong and hard to manage, having no bridle wisdom whatever, but he is of tough fibre and has a willing nature, and behind his mournful countenance there always seems to be lurking a crafty and elusive sense of humour. The names are marvellous. At the various stops on our way up the Nile I became personally acquainted with Rameses the Great, Rameses Telegraph, Rameses Telephone, Jim Corbett, Whiskey Straight, Lovely Sweet, Roosevelt, Sleeping Car, Lydia Pinkham, and others equally appropriate which I cannot now recall.

As I have indicated above, our wanderings have carried us as far as Luxor. Luxor (the ancient Thebes) is the superlative of all that is old and amazing in Egypt and therefore it calls for at least one separate chapter.

CHAPTER XVII

IN AND AROUND LUXOR, WITH A SIDE LIGHT ON RAMESES THE GREAT

UNTIL we arrived at Luxor we did not know the total meaning of the word " old." The ruins, which are the stock in trade of this ancient City of Thebes, date so far back into the dimness of Nowhere that all the other antiquities of earth seem as fresh and recent as a morning newspaper.

" Old " is merely a relative term, after all. I remember in my native town we small boys used to gaze in reverent awe at a court house that was actually built before the Civil War. We would look up at that weather-beaten frame structure, two stories high, with a square bird cage on top of it, and to us it had all the historic interest of a mediæval castle. Later, in Chicago, when the special writer on the newspaper ran short of topics he would dish up an illustrated story on the oldest building in town. It was constructed away back in 1833.

When a man from the West goes East for the first time and sees Independence Hall in Philadelphia, he

takes off his hat and tries to grasp the overwhelming fact that the building stood there even in the far
distant Colonial period. When he travels to London
and walks through St. Paul's or stands in the Henry
VII. Chapel at Westminster he begins to get a new
line on the meaning of " old." Later he sees the
Forum at Rome and declares to himself :—" At last
I have found something really ancient."

But when he arrives at Luxor and rambles among
the elephantine ruins and sits in the deep cool shade
of temples that had been standing a good many centuries before anyone thought of laying out the
Forum in Rome he will begin to understand how
everything else in the world is comparatively hot
from the griddle. One day we were in the shop of
Mouhammed Mouhassib, in Luxor, and the old
antiquarian reached under the counter and lugged
out a mummy. The body was well preserved, and the
embalming cloth in which it was wrapped and cross-
wrapped still retained a definite texture.

" This mummy dates back beyond any of the
dynasties of which we have a record," said the dealer.
" There were no inscriptions on the mummy case,
because when this gentleman lived it was not the
custom to inscribe the cocoon. You will observe,
however, that he was buried in a sitting posture, and

we know that this manner of burial was discontinued about 6000 B. C."

As we stood there gazing into the calm features of the unidentified has-been and realised that he had been sitting in that easy attitude for eight thousand years waiting for us to come along and be presented to him, we began to get a faint inkling of what the word " old " really means.

Goodness knows I am not going to attempt any detailed description of the stupendous ruins which make Luxor the most interesting spot in Egypt. Anyone who is going to describe Luxor needs a new box of adjectives every few minutes, and, besides, to repeat over and over again that the columns and cavernous sanctuaries at Karnak are " gigantic," and " colossal," and " huge," and so on, cannot bring the reader to any actual conception of the barbaric massiveness of these ancient structures.

The rulers who built the main temple of Karnak, a section at a time, thought they were not doing themselves credit unless they piled up columns about the size of the redwood trees in California and guarded each entrance with statues as big as the Goddess of Liberty in New York Harbour, and when they made a wall to enclose a courtyard, they put up something to resemble a mountain range. The ordinary 150 pound mortal edging his way through the corridors and under the vast shadows of these overwhelming uplifts of masonry feels about as large and as important as a gnat.

Everywhere about these temples there are uniformed guards whose duty it is to protect the remains against the vandal and the relic hunter. The guard follows a few feet behind you as you roam through the many acres of toppling ruin. He is afraid that you will steal something. Inasmuch as the smallest fragment of one of these huge statues, or obelisks, would weigh probably six hundred pounds, we felt that he was not justified in suspecting us. But he followed along and then, when we were leaving, he calmly came forward and indicated that he was ready to take a money insult. This move on his part was most characteristic of the Egyptian attitude toward visitors in general. Every native expects to get something out of a traveller for the simple reason that he needs the money. Suppose that a suspicious character should arrive in an American city and the chief of police sent out a detective to shadow him and see that he did not blow open any safes or crawl into any second stories. The detective, having followed the suspect all day, approaches him at nightfall and says, " Look here; you have put me to a lot of trouble. I have been on my feet all day watching you for fear that you were going to commit a burglary, and I think it is only right that you should pay me something."

Every time we visited an antiquity these guards tagged at our heels, watching us like hawks, and invariably they tried to hold us up for a piece of silver before we departed. There is a Masonic understanding among the natives that the tourist is to be fleeced. For instance, although the copper coins are in common use among the natives, and in the cheaper shops the prices are usually reckoned in milliemes, it is almost impossible for a traveller to get any of these copper coins because the natives want him to bestow his gratuities in piastres. A millieme is worth one-half cent, and then the millieme is further subdivided into fractional coins, some of which are about the size of the mustard seed and worth about as much as a share of mining stock.

Egyptian money is very easily understood by Americans. The piastre is the same as our five-cent piece or nickel. The silver five piastre piece resembles our quarter and has the same value. The ten piastre piece is the same as our half-dollar. The 100 piastre bill is worth five dollars. Inasmuch as many of the prices sound large and important when quoted in piastres, the dealers have learned to demand English pounds sterling or American dollars. That is, they name their first prices in sovereigns and dollars and then gradually work down to piastres. I saw a native trying to sell a scarab to a tourist. His first price was £7, equivalent to $35. After a half-hour of haggling he had cut it to 7 piastres, or 35 cents, and the deal was consummated.

The old city of Thebes was a huge and hustling metropolis, surrounded by a high wall of a hundred gates, with countless regiments of soldiers marching out to conquer distant lands and bring back slaves in little batches of 80,000 or so. This was along about 2000 B. C. The city began to lose some of its importance a few centuries before the Christian era and dwindled in size until twenty years ago it was a mere village of huts nestling in the shade of the great temples. Then the tourist travel set in very heavily, and to-day Luxor is a hustling city with large hotels and fancy shops and a general air of prosperity. The magnificent temple of Luxor is in the very heart of the new city. The rambling temple of Karnak is a short donkey ride to the north, and across the river, some three miles to the west, there are more temples and shattered statues

and the wonderful tombs of the kings. In olden days
there was a broad avenue leading north to Karnak
and thence west to the valley in the desert, where
the kings were buried, and this boulevard was
guarded on either side, for the entire distance, by
huge recumbent Sphinxes carved out of granite.
Can you imagine a double row of gigantic figures
crouched on each side of the street and about
twenty feet apart all the way up Broadway to Central Park and then through the Park to Riverside
Drive and up the drive to the distant suburbs? If
so, you will understand to what an extent these old
rulers " went in " for sphinxes. Labour cost nothing
and time did not count for anything and if a king
wished to build an avenue of sphinxes leading to his
private temple or tomb all he had to do was to give
the word.

As soon as a king mounted the throne he began
making his funeral preparations, and ordered the
entire staff of stone cutters to chisel out hieroglyphs
explaining that he was great and good and just,
and that he never took off his hat to anyone except
the gods, and then not ordinary picayune gods, but
only those of the very first magnitude. According
to the hieroglyphs, every king that ruled in Egypt
was as wise as Solomon, as brilliant in military

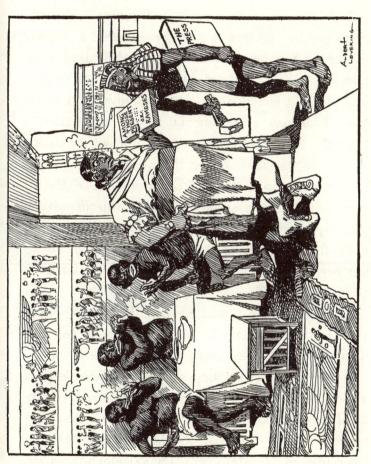

In old Egypt, every king was his own press agent

strategy as Napoleon, and as hard on the evildoer as our own beloved T. R.

This unanimous outpouring of eulogy is largely explained by the fact that every memorial in honour of a ruler was erected and supervised by that ruler himself. It's a fact! Of all the countless temples and obelisks and godlike granite figures and festal tomb chambers remaining in Egypt to testify to the majesty and splendour of the ancient dynasties, every one was built under the personal supervision of the man who gets all of the glory out of the inscriptions. The succeeding generation never got up subscription lists to build monuments to statesmen or military commanders. The dutiful and loving son never ordered a memorial in honour of his illustrious father. He was too busy carving his own biography on the sandstone and depicting himself as pursuing the enemy or taking afternoon tea with haughty three-headed gods.

In old Egypt every king was his own press agent. These rulers could have written some great " personal recollections " for the magazines, because they remembered all the incidents that brought them to the centre of the stage with the calcium turned on, and wisely forgot all details calculated to injure their standing with posterity.

IN AND AROUND LUXOR

You take Rameses the Great. He is regarded as perhaps the king pin of all the rulers during Egypt's long period of national splendour. Have you ever heard anyone say a word in criticism of Rameses' fiscal policy, his treatment of the rebate system, management of the Senate, or his social relations with the dark emissaries that came up from Nubia? No! Everyone has a good word for Rameses. The writers of ancient history extol him, and the guide books print his name in big black letters, and the travellers to Egypt gather about his glass-covered coffin in the Ghizeh Museum at Cairo and try to trace noble lineaments in the shrunken features. They sigh over his departure and look down at him mournfully, with their hats in their hands, as if they had lost him this spring, instead of 3164 years ago this spring. They say:—" Well, he certainly was a grand character and it's too bad we haven't got some rulers of his calibre nowadays."

It is not my desire to attack Rameses, but I feel it my duty to submit to students of history and archæologists a very interesting papyrus, which came into my possession at Luxor. If this document is accepted as authentic and the statements are believed, then it would appear that Rameses was the champion advertiser of ancient times. If Ram-

They look down at him mournfully

eses were alive to-day he would own all the bill-boards in America. He would take a full page in every Sunday paper and have his picture on free calendars. He would give Lawson cards and spades.

In all accepted records discovered up to this time Rameses has received nothing but praise. Why? Because all the records were doctored by Rameses himself. He was the great builder of Egypt and all over the walls of every building that he erected he had his picture and tales of his mighty achievements blazoned forth in bright colors like the row of ban-ners in front of a side show. Wherever in Egypt he could find a large smooth-faced rock he would engage a member of the Royal Academy to sculp something about Rameses, and he would always stand and look over the sculptor's shoulder to make sure that the king didn't get the worst of it. If the army of Ram-eses suffered a defeat at the hands of the Hittites, did any mention of the fact find its way into the inscriptions? Most assuredly not. Rameses had the hieroglyphs report that he made a masterly man-œuvre in order to develop the strength of the enemy and then retired to a new and more strategic position.

We cannot discover from the old inscrip-tions that any Egyptian army ever suffered defeat, and yet it has been learned from other sources that now and then an invading army had the whole native population running foot races up and down the Nile.

To make sure the King didn't get the worst of it

However, it was not considered good form for historians to mention these painful incidents. The rate of mortality among those who criticised the administration was exactly 100 per cent. It is because all of the familiar records are known to have been under censorship that the papyrus discovered by me at Luxor possesses a most startling interest.

As a cold matter of fact, I discovered this manuscript by proxy. That is, I bought it from the man who said he had found it concealed in the funeral vestments of a mummy uprooted near Thebes in the month of February. I cannot give the name of this Egyptian for the reason that all valuable antiquities discovered in Egypt are supposed to belong to the government, and anyone concealing an art treasure or some document of rare value may be severely punished. I can say this much, however—the native from whom I bought the papyrus assured me that he was an honourable and truthful guide, and he gave me his personal guarantee that he had removed the document from the mummy's undergarment with his own hands and had been waiting an opportunity to offer it to a traveller who was really a *connoisseur* of antiquities and a reverent student of ancient languages. All this he told me while we were out on the desert together, and after looking apprehensively in all directions to make sure that no human being was within three miles of us, he pulled a tin cylinder from under his robe and carefully removed from it the time-stained but still intact roll of papyrus. I must

say that I never saw a more convincing document.
The hieroglyphs looked as Egyptian as anything
could be, and as soon as I saw them I had a burning curiosity to know what message to future generations this poor mummy had been hugging in his
bosom through all these centuries. I asked regarding
the mummy on which the papyrus had been found
and learned that the inscription on his outer coffin
indicated that he had been an officer assigned to the
royal palace of Rameses II., the type of courtier
who must bend the supple knee and wear the smiling
face, at all times concealing his real opinion of things
in general.

The guarantee which accompanied the papyrus
was so heartfelt and altogether emphatic that I
made the purchase. The price was large, but I felt
justified in paying it, for the native assured me that
I could sell it to the British Museum at any time for
twice as much. I promised faithfully that I would
never mention his name in connection with the deal,
and this promise was easily kept, because he had a
name that no one could have remembered for two
minutes.

For obvious reasons I did not show the document
to my travelling companions. I knew that if people
heard of my discovery and got to talking about it

I might not be permitted to take it out of the country. When we arrived at Cairo I went to Mr. Ralph

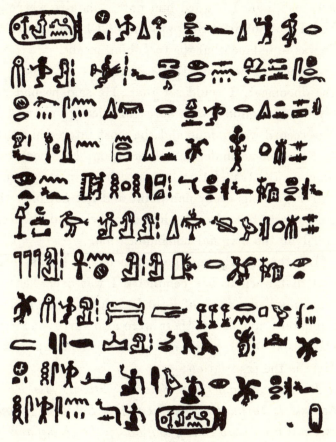

The original papyrus

Blanchard, an American who is noted as an antiquarian, Egyptologist, and mummy collector, and after a few cautious preliminaries told him that I had a document in hieroglyphics of which I desired a translation. I begged him not to inquire where or how I had obtained the papyrus. All I wanted him to do was to tell me what the fool thing meant.

Blanchard was startled as soon as he looked at the document. I could see that. He said he had deciphered a good many acres of hieroglyphics, but this record was unique and the most interesting that had ever come under his observation. He spent two days on the translation, so as to be absolutely accurate regarding every fine point and get not only the cold words but also the literary style and the real spirit of the original communication.

Let the translation speak for itself. I must confess that when it was completed I was overwhelmed. Not only had a flood of light been let in upon a most important epoch, but there were also surprising revelations as to the origin of valued words and phrases. Here is the translation:—

Rameses Second is a Smooth Citizen. His Foxy Scheme is to bunko Posterity. His Soldiers go out and put up a hard Scrap and do up the enemy and he hires a Stonecutter to give an Account of it on a Granite Rock and hand all the Bouquets to Rameses. He is building many Temples. The Architects draw the Plans. The Labourers do the Work. The Public foots the Bill. Rameses and the Local Deities are the only ones who butt into the Inscriptions. He has the future doped out as follows:—Three thousand years

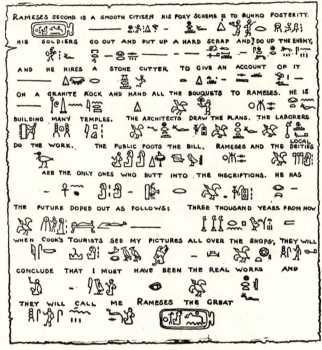

Translation of the Rameses papyrus

from now, when Cook's Tourists see my Pictures all over the Shop, they will conclude that I must have been the real Works and they will call me Rameses the Great.

259

This revelation in regard to the self-advertising proclivities of the great monarch, coming, as it did, from one who had been intimately associated with him, was so vastly important that Mr. Blanchard thought it better to verify the translation. He took a copy of the document to several eminent Egyptologists, and they agreed with him on every point. They said there was no getting away from " scraps " and " butt in " and " dope out " and other characters which seemed to me to have somewhat of a modern flavour.

After a man has been universally respected for nearly three thousand two hundred years it does seem a low down trick to show him up. And, possibly, the anonymous writer was prejudiced because he had failed to secure an appointment. Did the papyrus really come from the bosom of the mummy? Who knows? Sometimes it is the duty of the traveller to record facts as they come under his observation and not to draw hasty conclusions.

The documentary evidence is submitted herewith —first a copy of the original papyrus and then the translation, word for word and phrase by phrase. The testimony should convince any who are disposed to be sceptical. My only hope is that it will not entirely blast the reputation of Rameses.

CHAPTER XVIII

THE ORDINARY HUMAN FAILINGS OF THE ANCIENT MOGULS

TAKEN by themselves, as mere mouldering chunks of antiquity that have been preserved to us because they happened to be dropped down in a dry climate, the fragmentary remains of old Egypt are not very inspiring. They were big, but seldom beautiful. As records proving that humanity—old-fashioned, unreliable humanity, with its fears, jealousies, hatreds, and aching ambitions—is just about the same as it was five thousand years ago, the temples and the decorated tombs seem to bring us direct and heartfelt messages from our brethren of the long ago.

For instance, from the beginning of time probably the most maddening and unbearable persecution that can be visited upon a sensitive human being is to have some other human being always held up before him as a shining moral example.

Do you recall, O male reader, how you writhed in humiliation and laid plans for assault and battery when the good little Rollo of your native town was constantly dangled before your depraved soul as the paragon of juvenile virtues? " Rollo never smokes corn silk." " Rollo never puts tick-tacks on teacher's bedroom window." " Rollo never carries craw dab-

The paragon of juvenile virtues

bers in his Sunday clothes." " Rollo never runs away to go swimming and then comes back with his ears full of gravel."

No, indeed, Rollo never showed any of the traits

that have been the essence of boyhood since Adam and Eve started the original brood. And do you remember how bright and sunshiny that day seemed when Rollo, having grown to pale and sidewhiskered manhood, was arrested for stealing money from the Building and Loan Association?

Take the story of Queen Hatasoo. She was the Victoria of the eighteenth dynasty, and was on the throne just about 1500 B. C. The lineal male descendant of that period had a blot on the 'scutcheon or a bar sinister across his pedigree or something wrong with his registry certificate—anyway, he could not qualify as king, and so his sister Hatasoo was made ruler and he was permitted to hang around the palace as a kind of shawl holder and cab opener. He led the cotillons and attended public dinners and wore decorations, but Hatasoo ran Egypt and Thutmes Second was merely a trailer. When he dropped off there did not seem to be any considerable vacancy in court circles. Queen Hatasoo continued as chief monarch, although her step-nephew, Thutmes Third, carried the honourary title of co-regent. Hatasoo was energetic and ambitious. She put nephew into a remote back seat and ran things to suit herself, waging wars, building temples, and organising expeditions to far distant lands. Also, according to an-

263

cient custom, she had her portrait and the record of
her accomplishments carved on the obelisks and
painted all over the walls of her private temple,
which is still standing, about three miles west of the
present city of Luxor.

She reigned for thirty-five years, and then Thutmes Third, gray bearded and worn with much waiting, emerged from the nursery and took up the reins
of government. According to the judgment of later
historians, his reign was about the most glorious in
the whole history of Egypt. He was possessed of
military genius, and under his direction Syria was
recaptured, and the influence of Egypt was firmly
established in Western Asia. But no matter how
many battles he won or how many captives he brought
back to Thebes to exhibit in the courthouse square,
the old-timers around the court wagged their heads
and said, " Yes, he's doing fairly well for a begin-
ner, but he'll never come up to the mark set by his
Aunt Hattie." Hatasoo was her full name, but
those who had known her for a long time called her
" Hattie," and to a few of her intimates she was
known as " Hat."

Thutmes was merely human. For years his dom-
ineering aunt had kept him out of the running, and
now that he was on the throne the glory of her

achievements was constantly being dinged into him. Every time he rode out in his chariot, standing up and sawing away at four horses, just as they do

" He'll never come up to the mark set by his aunt Hattie "

in Ringling's circus at the present time, he saw her name and picture on all the public buildings, and, of course, two or three years after her departure, everybody bragged about her a good deal harder than they had while she was alive. Even the English news-

265

papers speak in kindly terms of an American states-
man who is safely deceased.

Thutmes stood it as long as he could, and then he
broke over. He ordered the stonecutters to go forth
and gouge out all the inscriptions relating to his
superior aunt. The temple which she had built as a
special memorial he appropriated to himself, and
put his name over the main entrance. It may have
been pretty spiteful, but the whole proceeding somehow seems to establish a sympathetic link between
those remote heathen days and the unselfish Utopian
civilisation that we now enjoy in Chicago, Omaha,
West Superior, and other centres of brotherly love.

After Thutmes had put in years erasing and chis-
elling out all complimentary references to Hatasoo, he passed away and was carried to a winding
subterranean tomb in the valley to the west. For
two hundred years the great monuments which he had
erected in his own honour, or quietly borrowed from
his aunt, remained intact. Then along came Rameses
Second, to whom we have already referred as the best
little advertiser of ancient times. He had the name
of Thutmes removed from all the temples, obelisks,
and public buildings, and put his own glaring label
on everything in sight. In the language of Mr.
Peasley, the Kings seemed to spend most of their

time in " knocking their predecessors " and " boost-
ing " themselves.

Nearly every ancient structure has been defaced

or altered to gratify a private jealousy or some
prejudice founded on religious belief. The Romans

tried to obliterate the old Egyptian deities. The early Christians hacked away at anything that failed to strike them as being orthodox. Then the Turks capped the climax by coming in and burning everything non-Mohammedan that was at all combustible. A few ancient records remain because they are carved in huge characters on very hard stone. The theologians wanted to batter them down, but it would have meant a lot of hard work and they had been leading sedentary lives. So they merely crisscrossed them and wrote the equivalent for "Rats" underneath, and let it go at that.

Even the modern circus bill is not more exuberant and given to joyful hyperbole than the inscriptions and paintings of the Egyptian temples. A few of them are reproduced herewith. Take No. 1, for example. This represents our old friend Rameses the Great in the act of overcoming his enemies. It was designed by Rameses himself. Now we know where Kaiser Wilhelm got all of his tips.

Some warriors are content with overcoming one man at a time, but Rameses is seen holding ten of them by the hair, getting ready to clout them into insensibility. The picture is an artistic success, but is somewhat shy anatomically. The ten enemies have a total of only three legs for the whole crowd. They are better supplied with arms, the total being thirteen, or about one and one-third to the man. Notice also the relative size of Rameses and his foes. There

Where Kaiser Wilhelm got all his tips

we have the real, unchanging spirit of autobiography—the great I triumphant and the petty antagonists all coming about knee high to him.

No. 2 is also very characteristic. One of the kings is represented as defeating two burly warriors. He is walking on one and pushing his spear through the other. Undoubtedly a glorious achievement. It would

be still more glorious if the two gentlemen putting
up the fight against the King had carried weapons
of some sort. The one on the ground, who is lifting
his hands in mild protest against being used as a
rug, has nothing on his person to indicate that he is
a soldier. The one who is being harpooned carries in
his left hand what appears to be a box of handkerchiefs. The raised right arm would suggest that
he attempted to slap the King, who caught him by
the arm and held him until he could select a good
vital spot in which to prong him. Attention is called
to the fact that both of the victims wear the long
and protuberant chin whisker, which would indicate
that the honest farmer was getting the worst of it
even four thousand years ago.

The carvings and paintings which do not depict
warlike scenes usually show the monarchs receiving
homage from terrified subjects or else mingling on
terms of equality with the principal deities of the
period. Illustration No. 3 is a very good specimen.
King Amenophis and his wife are seen seated on
their square-built Roycroft thrones, while two head
priests of Ammon burn incense before them and sing
their praises and tell them that the people are with
the administration, no matter how the Senate may
carry on. There was no race prejudice in those days.

The Queen is shown to be a coal-black Nubian. In one hand she carries what seems to be a fly brush of the very kind that we used all the time we were up the Nile, and if the article in her other hand is not a cocktail glass then the artist has wilfully libelled her.

No. 4 is interesting as a fashion plate. Ptolemeus and Cleopatra are making offers to the hawk-headed god and the goddess Hathor. This picture will appeal to women inasmuch as it gives us a correct likeness of Cleopatra, the man trapper. No one can dispute the fact that she is beautiful, but how about the combination of an Empress gown with a habit back? Is it not a trifle daring? And the hat. Would you call it altogether subdued?

Another well-preserved painting to be found in the temple at Edfou reveals the innate modesty of the Ptolemies. The King (No. 5) is represented as being crowned by the goddesses of the south and the north —that is, of Upper and Lower Egypt. These divinities seem to be overcome with admiration of the athletic monarch. One has her hand resting on his shoulder, as if she hated to see him go. The other, having just fitted him with his new gourd-shaped hat, has both hands in the air, and you can almost hear her say, " Oh, my! It looks just fine!"

Seti **I.** was another shrinking violet. In one of his private three-sheet advertisements (No. **6**) he has the sublime effrontery to represent the great goddess Hathor as holding his hand tenderly and offering him the jewelled collar which she is wearing. Notice the uplifted hand. He is supposed to be saying, " This is all very sudden, and besides, would it be proper for me to accept jewelry from one of your sex? " Of course, there never was any Hathor, and if there had been she wouldn't have hob-nobbed with a man who had his private interviews done into oil paintings. But this painting and one thousand others that we have seen in Egypt help to give us a line on the ancient Kings. If there was any one of them that failed to get the swelled head soon after mounting the throne, the hieroglyphs are strangely silent regarding his case. They were a vain, self-laudatory lot, and all of them had that craving for the centre of the stage and the hot glare of the spot-light which is still to be found in isolated cases.

After all is said and done can we blame them? Rameses wanted to be remembered and talked about and he laid his plans accordingly. He carved the record of his long and successful reign on the unyielding granite and distributed his pictures with the careful prodigality of a footlight favourite. What has been the result? His name is a household joke all over the world. People who never heard of Professor Harry Thurston Peck or Marie Corelli or the present Khedive of Egypt know all about Rameses the Great, although no two of them pronounce it the same.

CHAPTER XIX

ROYAL TOMBS AND OTHER PLACES OF AMUSEMENT

ONE morning we rode across the Nile from Luxor in a broad and buxom sailboat, climbed on our donkeys, and rode to the west. We followed the narrow road through the fresh fields of wheat and alfalfa until we struck the desert, and then we took to a dusty trail which leads to a winding valley, where the kings of the eighteenth, nineteenth, and twentieth dynasties are being dug up.

This narrow valley, with the steep hills rising on either side, is the sure-enough utterness of desolation; not a tree, not a shrub, not a blade of grass, not even a stingy little cactus. No wonder the old kings picked out this valley for a cemetery. Life has no charm in this dreary region. Eternal sleep would seem to offer peculiar advantages. After winding through the sun-baked gravel for about a mile we came to a settlement of houses and a high fence

274

thrown across the roadway. Also there was an electric light plant buzzing away merrily. The tombs of the kings are now strung with incandescent lights. Can you beat that for sacrilegious enterprise?

There are forty-one of these royal tombs that have been discovered and opened to date. The less important are not lighted, and are mere tunnels leading back to one or two bare chambers. Those really worth visiting are dug far back into the hills. The halls are spacious and brilliantly decorated, and before you get through exploring one of them you think that you are pretty well down toward the centre of the earth.

Mr. Peasley had read up on the Tomb of Amenhotep Third and when we entered it he pushed the regular guide out of the way and gave us one of his own vivid lectures. The native guide lacks imagination. His idea of showing the traveller a frolicsome time is to point out a lot of paintings in which the deceased is seen travelling across the Nile in a funeral barge. Mr. Peasley, on the other hand, gave us an insight into the character of the wily Amenhotep.

" Now, look at the entrance to this tomb," he said, as we started down the new wooden steps. " It looks as if someone had been blasting for limestone. The

walls are rough and unfinished. Old Amenhotep figured that if anyone ever came across the opening to
the tomb he would size up this ordinary hole in the
ground and conclude that it was either a cave used

" Now look at the entrance to this tomb," he said

as a storehouse or the last resting place of some
cheap two-dollar official."

After descending some twenty feet we came to a
small chamber which was rudely frescoed about half
of the way around.

" Do you know why he left this job unfinished? "

asked Mr. Peasley. " He knew that some day or other an inquisitive foreigner would be prowling around here trying to uncover ancient treasures, and he put this measly little antechamber here to throw Mr. Archæologist off the scent. He wanted it to appear that the man who was buried here had been so poor that he couldn't complete the decorations. And now I'll show you something more foxy still. Come with me down this long flight of steps to the second chamber."

He led us down another flight to a tall chamber about the size of a freight car stood on end.

" When the French explorers opened this place in 1898 the chamber which you are now inspecting seemed to be the end of the tunnel," continued Mr. Peasley. " The four side walls were perfectly smooth and unbroken, but down at the bottom they found a pit which had been filled with heavy stones. They supposed, of course, that this was the mummy pit, and that if they removed the stones they would find some royal remains at the other end of the hole. So they worked day after day, lifting out the boulders, and finally they came to the end of the pit and found that they had drawn a blank. Naturally they were stumped. They thought they had been exploring a tomb, but it was only an April fool joke. One

of the professors was not satisfied. He felt sure that
there must be a royal mummy tucked in somewhere
about the premises, so he took a ladder and climbed
around and began tapping all over the walls of this
second chamber. What do you think? He discovered
that the wall had a hollow sound just opposite the
tunnel at which they had entered. So he used a bat-
tering ram and broke through into the real tomb.
Yes, sir; these two outer chambers, with their cheap
stencil frescoes and fake mummy pit, had been a
blind."

We passed over a narrow wooden bridge and entered the tunnel beyond the second chamber. The
whole place was brightly illuminated and one could
readily believe that he was in a modern hallway
decorated in the most gorgeous Egyptian style.
The bordering frescoes and the historical paintings
were as fresh in tone as if they had been put on
only yesterday. One of the larger chambers looked
exactly like the gaudy " Oriental apartment " of a
Paris or New York hotel, and we shouldn't have been
surprised or displeased to see a waiter come in with
a tray full of cool drinks.

At last we came to the tomb chamber, and there in
a deep hollow, with a modern wooden railing around
it, reclined the great King Amenhotep, with the in-

candescent lamps dangling above him and flooding him in a radiant light. The original granite cover of the outer case has been removed and plate glass substituted. We leaned on the rail and gazed down at the serene countenance of the once mighty monarch who had been lying there for 3300 years. The funeral garlands which had been laid on his breast were still undisturbed, and the shrunken face was illumined by that calm smile of triumph which Amenhotep wore when he passed away confident in the belief that the Nile tourist would never discover his hiding place.

We visited the tomb in company with a bustling swarm of American excursionists of the happy, irreverent kind. The fact that they were strolling about in a private and highly aristocratic sarcophagus did not seem to repress their natural gush of spirits or induce any solemn reflections. They were all steaming hot, but very happy and having a lot of fun with the King. One enterprising Yankee, who carried his coat and vest on his arm, started to climb over the wooden railing in order to make a close inspection of the mortuary remains, but was restrained by the guards.

After leaving the valley of tombs we made a short cut over a very hot and a very high hill to the " rest house " which has been erected far out on the desert by one of the tourist agencies. We collapsed on the shady side of the building, dusty and short of breath, and immediately we were attacked by a most vociferous horde of native peddlers. And what do you suppose they were selling? We landed there on Friday, and the remnant sale of mummies was in full blast. Here are some of the cut prices:—

Head of adult...................... 4 *shillings.*
Foot of adult .... 1 *shilling.*
Hand of adult .... 1 *shilling.*
Two feet and two hands (warranted
  mates) .... 3 *shillings.*
Arm and head ....6 *shillings.*
Special reduction for juvenile sizes.

Can you imagine anything more disquieting to the nerves, when you are resting and getting ready for luncheon, than to have a villainous child of the desert rush up and lay a petrified human head in your lap and beg you to make an offer? Within two minutes after we arrived we had fragments of former humanity stacked all around us. And they were unmistakably genuine. The native swindlers can make imitation scarabs and potteries, or else import them by the gross from Germany and Connecticut, but the mummy heads which they offer for sale are horribly bona fide. It would not pay to manufacture an imitation article, inasmuch as the whole desert region

For the loved ones at home

to the west of ancient Thebes is a vast cemetery. If the merchant's stock runs low he can go out with a spade and dig up a new supply, just as a farmer would go after artichokes.

Our guide co-operated with the ghouls. He rushed
about hunting up strange and grisly specimens and
brought them to us and begged us to examine them
and then pick out a few for the loved ones at home.
I regret to say that we did purchase a few of these
preserved extremities. The guide said we could use
them as paper weights.

This same dragoman, or guide, or highbinder, or
whatever you may choose to call him—and Mr. Peasley called him nearly everything—gave us a lot of
cheerful entertainment during our four days in
Luxor. Mr. Peasley was in hot pursuit of guaranteed antiquities. He said he had an old bookcase at
home which he was going to convert into a curio
cabinet. There is one dealer in Luxor who is said to
be absolutely trustworthy. He supplies museums and
private collections throughout the world, and if you
buy a scarab or a carved image from him you know
that you have something genuine and worth keeping.
Mr. Peasley in a thoughtless moment requested the
dragoman to conduct us to this shop. We went in
and burrowed through the heaps of tempting rubbish
and began to dicker for a job lot of little images,
tear jars, amulets, etc., that are found in the mummy
cases. That dragoman saw the covetous gleam in the
Peasley eye and he knew that the man from Iowa in-

tended loading up with antiques, and he also knew that Mr. Peasley wished to do this purchasing single-handed and without the assistance of a dragoman, who would come in for a ten per cent. commission. We told the dealer we would drop around later. So we went to the hotel and dismissed the dragoman— told him to go home and get a good night's rest and be on hand at nine o'clock the next morning.

After we were safely in the hotel Mr. Peasley confided his plans to us.

" I don't want to buy the stuff while that infernal Mahmoud is along," he said. " Why should he get a rake-off? We didn't go to the shop on his recommendation. Now, I'll go over there by myself, pick out what I want, and strike a bargain."

We offered to go along and assist, so we started up a side street, and after we had gone a block Mahmoud stepped out from a doorway and said, " Come, I will show you the way." We told him we had just sauntered out for a breath of air, so we walked aimlessly around a block and were escorted back to the hotel.

" I'll go over the first thing in the morning," said Mr. Peasley. " I'll be there at eight o'clock, because he isn't due here until nine."

When he arrived at the shop early next morning

Mahmoud was standing in the doorway wearing a grin of devilish triumph. Mr. Peasley kept on walking and pretending not to see him, but he **came back** to the hotel mad all the way through.

"We're up against an Oriental mind-reader, but I'll fool him yet," he declared. "When we come

Mahmoud—wearing a grin of devilish triumph

back to the hotel for luncheon and he is waiting for us with the donkey boys on the east side of the hotel we will go out the west door to the river bank and cut south around the Presbyterian Mission and come back to the shop."

Mr. Peasley did not know that Mahmoud had organised all the hotel servants into a private detective agency. He must have known of our escape on the river side before we had gone a hundred feet from the hotel, for when, after executing our brilliant flank movement, we arrived at the shop of the antiquarian, Mahmoud and the proprietor were sitting in the front room drinking Turkish coffee and waiting for the prey to wander into the trap. Mahmoud did not seem surprised to see us. He bade us welcome and said that his friend the dealer was an Egyptologist whose guarantee was accepted by every museum in the world, and if we were in the market for antiques he would earnestly advise us to seek no further. After this evidence of a close and friendly understanding between the dragoman and the dealer we had a feeling that Mahmoud would get his ten per cent, even if we succeeded in eluding him and buying on our own hook.

But we hated to acknowledge ourselves beaten. At dusk that evening we started toward the shop, in a half-hearted and experimental spirit, and presently we observed Mahmoud following along fifty feet behind us. We went to the garden of a neighbouring hotel and sat there until eleven o'clock. When we came out Mahmoud was at the gateway. He said it was not always safe for travellers to be about the streets at night, so he would protect us and show us the way back to our hotel.

We found it impossible to get away from him. No Siberian bloodhound ever followed a convict's trail more closely. If we ventured forth, early or late, we found ourselves shadowed by that smiling reprobate. When it came to the last day in Luxor Mr. Peasley did the bold thing. He permitted Mahmoud to escort him to the shop, and then he said to the dealer:—" This man is our guide, but he is not entitled to any commission because he did not bring us to your shop. If he had recommended your shop in the first place we would not have come here at all. He is a bluff. He is trying to ring in. I want to buy a few things here, with the understanding that he doesn't get anything out of it. We have already paid him two salaries for guiding us and he isn't a guide at all—he's a night watchman."

The dealer vowed and protested that he never paid commissions to anyone. Mahmoud, not at all ruffled by the attack on his character, said that his only ambition in life was to serve the noble gentleman from the famous country known as Iowa. So Mr.

Peasley bought his assortment of antiques, and Mahmoud looked on and then carried the parcel back to the hotel, walking respectfully behind the " noble gentleman."

" Well, I blew myself," reported Mr. Peasley. " And I'll bet a thousand dollars that Mahmoud gets his ten per cent."

Whereupon Mahmoud smiled—the pensive, patronising smile of a civilisation five thousand years old looking down on the aboriginal product of the Western prairies.

On the morning of our departure from Luxor Mahmoud came around for his letter of recommendation. I had worked for an hour to write something evasive which would satisfy him and not perjure me too deeply. When he came to the hotel I gave him the following:—

To Whom It May Concern:—The bearer, Mahmoud, has been our dragoman for four days and has attended us faithfully at all hours; also, he has shown us as many temples as we wished to see.

He looked at the paper blankly and said, " I do not read English." At that Mr. Peasley brightened up. He read the testimonial aloud to Mahmoud and declared that it was incomplete and unworthy of the subject matter. In ten minutes he completed the following and the dragoman took it away with him, highly pleased:—

To Whom It May Concern—Greeting:—The bearer, Mahmoud, is a dragoman of monumental mendacity and commercial Machiavellism. His simulated efforts to faithfully serve us and protect our interests have had an altogether negative effect. Anyone employing him will find him possessed of moral turpitude and a superlative consciousness of his own worth. His knowledge of Egyptian history is enormously inconsequential, while his English vocabulary is amazing in its variety of verbal catastrophes. We commend him to travellers desirous of studying the native characteristics of the most geological stratum of society.

" He has made a lot of trouble for us, and now we've got even by ruining him," said Mr. Peasley.

It seemed a joke at the time, but later on, when we thought it over, we felt sorry for Mahmoud and wished we had not taken such a mean advantage of him. After all is said and done, a man must make a living.

On our way back to Cairo from Assouan we stopped over at Luxor. Mahmoud, by intuition or through telepathy, knew that we were coming and met us at the station. He was overjoyed to see us again.

"I showed your letter to a gentleman from the Kingdom of Ohio," said he, "and it procured for me one of the best jobs I ever had."

IN CAIRO

CHAPTER XX

MR. PEASLEY AND HIS FINAL SIZE-UP OF EGYPT

ON the morning of our hurried pack up and get away from Luxor we lost Mr. Peasley. It was a half-hour before the sailing of the boat, and we were attempting to lock trunks, call in the porters, give directions as to forwarding mail, and tip everybody except the proprietor all at the same time.

This excruciating crisis comes with every departure. The fear of missing the boat, the lurking suspicion that several articles have been left in lower drawers or under the sofa, the dread of overlooking some worthy menial who is entitled to baksheesh, the uneasy conviction that the bill contains several overcharges—all these combine to produce a mental condition about halfway between plain " rattles " and female hysteria. And then, to add to the horror of the situation, Mr. Peasley had disappeared.

All hands were needed—one to boss the porters, another to round up the tippees, another to audit the charges for " extras," another to make a final search for razor strops and hot water bags (of which we had left a trail from Chicago to Cairo). Instead of attending to these really important duties we were loping madly about the hotel looking for Peasley. We asked one another why we had invited him to join the party. We called him all the names that we had invented on the trip to fit his unusual personality. One of these was a " flat-headed fush." I don't know know what a " fush " is, but the more you study it and repeat it over to yourself, the more horrible becomes the full significance of the word. Also we called him a " swozzie," which means a chump who has gone on and on, exploring the furthermost regions of idiocy, until even his most daring companions are left far behind. We called Mr. Peasley a " wall-eyed spingo," the latter being a mullet that has lost all sense of shame. Ordinary abuse and profanity became weak and ineffective when pitted against words of this scathing nature.

Reader, if you have a life-long friend and you feel reasonably sure that you never could quarrel with him or be out of patience with him or find fault with any of his small peculiarities, go on a long trip with him in foreign lands. You will be together so much of the time that finally each will begin to hate the sight of the other. There will come off days, fraught with petty annoyances, when each will have a fretful desire to hurl cameras and suit cases at his beloved playmate. Suppose your lifelong friend has some little eccentricity of manner or speech, some slight irregularity of behaviour at the table, or a per-

You discover every one of his shining faults

verted and stubborn conviction which reveals itself in every controversy. You may have overlooked this defect for years because you meet him only at intervals, but when you begin to camp with him you discover every one of his shining faults. And how they

295

do get on your nerves! Next to matrimony, perhaps travelling together is the most severe test of compatibility.

We liked Mr. Peasley. Looking back over the trip, we can well believe that the expedition would have been rather tame if deprived of his cheering presence. But he was so full of initiative and so given to discovering byways of adventure that he was always breaking in on the programme and starting little excursions of his own. He was a very hard man to mobilise. If we had solemnly agreed to get together for luncheon at one o'clock, three of us would be waiting at the food garage while Mr. Peasley would be a mile away, trying to buy a four-dollar Abyssinian war shield for $2.75.

And where do you suppose he was on the morning we were making our frenzied departure from Luxor? We found him in the barber shop, having his hair cut. A native stood alongside of him, brushing away the flies. The barber, a curly Italian, had ceased work when we came in, and, encouraged by the questions of Mr. Peasley, was describing the Bay of Naples, pointing out Capri, Sorrento, Vesuve, and other points of interest, with a comb in one hand and a pair of scissors in the other. This barber had made an indelible impression on Mr. Peasley, because of his name, which was Signor Mosquito. Mr. Peasley said he didn't see how anyone with a name like that could live.

We lined up in front of Mr. Peasley and gazed at him in withering silence. He was not feazed.

"Talk about oriental luxury," he said. "Little did I think twenty years ago, when I was measurin'

He was not feazed

unbleached muslin and drawin' New Orleans syrup in a country store, that one day I'd recline on a spotted divan and have a private vassal to keep the flies off of me. To say nothing of bein' waited on by Signor Mosquito."

I tried to hold down the safety valve of my wrath.

"We have just held a meeting and by unanimous vote we have decided that you are an irresponsible fush, a night blooming swozzie, and a vitrified spingo," I said.

"Thanks," he replied. "I'll do as much for you sometime."

"Are you aware of the fact that the boat departs in twenty minutes?" asked No. 2.

"The boat will not leave its mooring until Peasley, of Iowa, is safely aboard," he replied. "Why is it that you fellows begin to throw duck fits every time we have to catch a boat or train? Kindly send my luggage aboard, and as soon as Signor Mosquito has concluded his amputations, I shall join you."

Words failed us. We hurried to the boat, feeling reasonably certain that he would follow us to As-souan by rail. When it came time to cast off, Mr. Peasley had not appeared, and our irritation was gradually softening into a deep joy. The warning whistle blew twice, and then Mr. Peasley came down the bank, carrying a Nubian spear eight feet long over his shoulder. By the time he had arrived on the upper deck the gangplank was drawn and we were swinging in the current.

He bestowed on us a cool smile of triumph, and then removed his hat. His hair had been given a shellac finish and smelled like the front doorway of a drug store.

" Signor Mosquito is well named," said Mr. Peasley. " When he got through with me he stung me for fifteen piastres."

For several hours we refused to speak to him or sit near him on deck, but finally we needed him to fill out a four-handed game of dominoes and he was taken back on probation. While we were engaged in a very stubborn session of " double nines," we noticed that most of our fellow passengers, and especially those of English persuasion, were making our little group the target for horrified glances. Some of them actually glared at us. We began to wonder if dominoes was regarded as an immoral practice in Egypt.

" These people keep on looking at us as if we were a happy band of burglars," said Mr. Peasley. " We think we are travelling incog., but our reputation has preceded us."

Then we heard one old lady ask another if there would be any evening services in the dining saloon,

and Mr. Peasley, who was reaching into the " bone
yard," suddenly paused with his hand up and exclaimed:—" Sanctified catfish! Boys, it's Sunday!"

" Boys, it's Sunday!"

It was. We had been sitting there among those
nice people throughout the calm Sabbath afternoon
playing a wicked game of chance. After two weeks
among the Mohammedans and other heathen, with
every day a working day and the English Sunday a dead letter, we had lost all trace of dates. Mr.

300

Peasley said that if anyone had asked him the day of the week he would have guessed Wednesday.

This unfortunate incident helped to deepen and solidify the dark suspicion with which we, as Americans, were regarded by the contingent from Great Britain. If our conduct had been exemplary we could not have cleared away this suspicion, but after the domino debauch we were set down as hopeless. The middle class English guard their social status very carefully, and you can't blame them. It is a tender and uncertain growth that requires looking after all the time. If they didn't water it and prune it and set it out in the sunshine every day it would soon wither back to its original stalk.

Did you ever come across a bunch of melancholy pilgrims from the suburban villas and the dull gray provincial towns of dear old England? Did you ever observe the frightened manner in which they hold aloof from Germans, Americans, Bedouins, Turks, and other foreigners? They fear that if they drift into friendly relationship with people they meet while travelling, later on some of these chance acquaintances may look them up at Birmingham or Stoke-on-Trent and expect to be entertained at the foundry.

A large majority of our fellow passengers from

Luxor to Assouan were of elderly pattern. We estimated the average age to be about eighty-three. Mr. Peasley said an irreverent thing about these venerable tourists.

"Why do these people come all the way to Egypt to look at the ruins?" he asked. "Why don't they stay at home and look at one another?"

We rebuked him for saying it, but somehow or other these rebukes never seemed to have any permanent restraining effect.

Our boat arrived at Assouan one morning accompanied by a sand storm and a cold wave. The Cataract Hotel stood on a promontory overlooking a new kind of Nile—a swift and narrow stream studded with gleaming boulders of granite. We liked Assouan because the weather was ideal (after the sand storm ran out of sand), the hotel was the best we had found in Egypt, and there were so few antiques that sightseeing became a pleasure. Besides, after one has been to Luxor, anything in the way of ancient temples is about as much of a come-down as turkey hash the day after Thanksgiving.

Here, on the border of Nubia, we began to get glimpses of real Africa. We rode on camels to a desert camp of hilarious Bisharins. They are the gypsies of Nubia—dress their hair with mud instead of bay rum and reside under a patch of gunnysack propped up by two sticks. On the hills back of the town we saw the barracks where the English army gathered itself to move south against the Mahdists. We were invited to go out in the moonlight and hunt hyenas, but did not think it right to kill off all the native game.

The big exhibit at Assouan, and one of the great engineering achievements of modern times, is the dam across the Nile. It is a solid wall of granite, a mile and a quarter long, 100 feet high in places and 88 feet through the base, and it looks larger than it sounds. We went across it on a push car after taking a boat ride in the reservoir basin, which is said to contain 234,000,000 gallons of water. This estimate is correct, as nearly as we could figure it. The dam is about four miles above the town. We rode up on a dummy train, with cars almost as large as Saratoga trunks, and came back in a small boat. We shot the rapids, just for excitement, and after we had caved in the bottom of the boat and stopped an hour for repairs we decided that we had stored up enough excitement, so after that we followed the more placid waters.

The black boatmen had a weird chant, which they repeated over and over, keeping time with the

stroke. It was a combination of Egyptian melody
and American college yell, and ran as follows:—

> Hep! Hep! Horay!
> Hep! Hep! Horay!
> Hep! Hep! Horay!
> All right! Thank you!

This effort represented their sum total of English,
and they were very proud of it, and we liked it, too
—that is, the first million times. After that, the
charm of novelty was largely dissipated.

Many people visit Assouan because of the kiln-
dried atmosphere, which is supposed to have a dis-
couraging effect on rheumatism and other ailments
that flourish in a damp climate. Assouan is as dry
as Pittsburg on Sunday. It is surrounded by desert
and the sun always seems to be working overtime.
The traveller who does much rambling out of doors
gradually assumes the brown and papery complex-
ion of a royal mummy, his lips become parched and
flaky, and he feels like a grocery store herring,
which, it is believed, is about the driest thing on
record.

We did love Assouan. Coming back from a camel
ride, with a choppy sea on, gazing through the heat
waves at the tufted palms and the shimmering white

walls, we would know that there was ice only a mile ahead of us, and then our love for Assouan would become too deep for words.

Burton Holmes, the eminent lecturer and travelogue specialist, was lying up at Assouan, having a tiresome argument with the germ that invented malaria. He had come up the Nile in a deep draught boat and had succeeded in finding many sand bars that other voyagers had overlooked. Just below Assouan the boat wedged itself into the mud and could not be floated until thirty natives, summoned from the surrounding country, had waded underneath and "boosted" all afternoon. When it came time to pay the men the captain of the boat said to Mr. Holmes: "What do you think? They demand eight shillings."

"It is an outrage," said Mr. Holmes. "Eight shillings is two dollars. Even in America I can get union labour for two dollars a day. There are thirty of them. Couldn't we compromise for a lump sum of fifty dollars?"

"You do not understand," said the captain. "We are asked to pay eight shillings for the whole crowd. I think that six would be enough."

Whereupon Mr. Holmes gave them ten shillings, or 8 1-3 cents each, and as he sailed away the grateful assemblage gave three rousing cheers for Mr. Rockefeller.

When we left Assouan we scooted by rail direct to Cairo, to rest up and recover from our recuperation.

It is customary in winding up a series of letters

to draw certain profound conclusions and give hints to travellers who may hope to follow the same beaten path. Fortunately, Mr. Peasley had done this for us. He promised a real estate agent in Fairfield, Iowa, that he would let him know about Egypt. One night in Assouan he read to us the letter to his friend, and we borrowed it:—

Assouan, Some time in April.

Deloss M. Gifford,
   Fairfield, Iowa, U. S. A.
My Dear Giff:—

I have gone as far up the Nile as my time and the letter of credit will permit. At 8 G. M. to-morrow I turn my face toward the only country on earth where a man can get a steak that hasn't got goo poured all over it. Meet me at the station with a pie. Tell mother I am coming home to eat.

Do I like Egypt? Yes—because now I will be satisfied with Iowa. Only I'm afraid that when I go back and see 160 acres of corn in one field I won't believe it. Egypt is a wonderful country, but very small for its age. It is about as wide as the court house square, but it seems to me at least 10,000 miles long, as we have been two weeks getting up to the First Cataract. Most of the natives are farmers. The hard-working tenant gets one-tenth of the crop every year and if he looks up to see the steamboats go by he is docked. All Egyptians who are not farmers are robbers. The farmers live on the river. All other natives live on the tourists.

307

IN PASTURES NEW

I have seen so many tombs and crypts and family vaults that I am ashamed to look an undertaker in the face. For three weeks I have tried to let on to pretend to make a bluff at being deeply interested in these open graves. Other people gushed about them and I was afraid that if I didn't trail along and show some sentimental interest they might suspect that I was from Iowa and was shy on soulfulness. I'll say this much, however —I'm mighty glad I've seen them, because now I'll never have to look at them again.

Egypt is something like the old settler—you'd like to roast him and call him down, but you hate to jump on anything so venerable and weak. Egypt is so old that you get the headache trying to think back. Egypt had gone through forty changes of administration and was on the down grade before Iowa was staked out.

The principal products of this country are insects, dust, guides, and fake curios. I got my share of each. I am glad I came, and I may want to return some day, but not until I have worked the sand out of my ears and taken in two or three county fairs. I have been walking down the main aisle with my hat in my hand so long that now I am ready for something lively.

Americans are popular in Egypt, during business hours. Have not been showered with social attentions, but I am always comforted by the thought that the exclusive foreign set cannot say anything about me that I haven't already said about it. Of course, we could retaliate in proper fashion if we could lure the foreigners out to Iowa, but that seems out of the question. They think Iowa is in South America.

I shall mail this letter and then chase it all the way home.

Give my love to everybody, whether I know them or not. Yours,   PEASLEY.

P. S.—Open some preserves.

Not a comprehensive review of the fruits of our journey and yet fairly accurate.

THE END